Lane has no idea what happened when he opens his eyes after dying. Finding out he's in the underworld is unexpected and unwelcome, but meeting the Egyptian god of the underworld, Osiris, soothes some of those feelings. Lane doesn't know where his place is, but he wouldn't mind if it were by Osiris's side.

Osiris and the entire Egyptian pantheon are in trouble, so it's not the best moment for Osiris to start a relationship with one of his dead souls — or maybe it is. Osiris will fight Apophis if he manages to break out of the darkness, and Lane gives him one more reason to stand strong.

The darkness is breaking, and Apophis is growing stronger. Will the gods be enough to stop him from leaving his prison? What will happen if they're not?

Last Bastion
Copyright © 2023 Catherine Lievens
ISBN: 978-1-4874-3942-2
Cover art by Angela Waters

Published by eXtasy Books Inc

Look for us online at:
www.eXtasybooks.com

LAST BASTION
FOR THE GODS' AMUSEMENT 5

BY

CATHERINE LIEVENS

CHAPTER ONE

When Lane opened his eyes, it took him a moment to realize he was dead.

He stared at the white ceiling, trying to get his thoughts into order. The last thing he remembered was getting stabbed in the side before falling to the ground. He lowered a hand to touch the wound, anticipating blood and gore.

The pain was gone. The street where he'd been lying was gone, too, and the only thing he could see was the white ceiling.

He sat up. He could tell he wasn't in a hospital, even though from where he was, he could see rows of simple beds with people lying on them. There were no medical instruments or doctors. The only people Lane could see who weren't in the same situation were guards at the open door. Their skin was dark, and they wore white gowns. Lane blinked at the sight of swords and spears.

What the fuck had happened?

"How did you die?" a male voice asked.

Lane looked around. The bed to his left was empty, but a man was stretched out on the bed to his right. He looked at ease, as if he knew what was happening, and Lane wanted to know, too.

"Who are you?" he asked.

The man grinned and sat up. "My name is Barnaby."

Lane nodded. Barnaby was cute, with green eyes sparkling behind his glasses and floppy brown hair hiding most of his forehead. He looked like he knew what was going on, so Lane swung his legs over the side of the bed and turned in Barnaby's direction.

Barnaby did the same, putting his elbows on his knees.

"I'm Lane," Lane said. "You know where we are?"

Barnaby shrugged a shoulder. "Underworld. I'm not entirely sure which one, but from the guards, I'm pretty sure it's Egyptian."

Lane blinked. He hadn't expected to end up in the Egyptian underworld when he died, but it was as good an underworld as any other. Unless people had a specific faith that was important to them, they were sorted into the various underworlds. Where they ended up didn't make any difference. They were dead, and that was that.

Lane touched his side again. He'd been stabbed, but that was the only thing he was sure of right now. Well, that and the fact that he was dead. He wouldn't be in the underworld if he weren't.

"How did you die, then?" Barnaby asked, leaning closer as if he expected to see a wound.

Lane dropped his hand. "I was mugged and stabbed, or at least, I think that's what happened. What about you?"

Barnaby shook his head, clearly not intending to tell Lane what had happened to him. It made Lane want to push, but it was none of his business. He and Barnaby had just met. They weren't friends, and it was okay for Barnaby to have secrets. Still, Lane didn't miss the way Barnaby reached for his throat for a moment. It made him wonder if maybe he'd been strangled. It wasn't something he wanted to think about, and if that was what had happened, he understood why Barnaby didn't want to explain himself.

"Do you know anything at all?" Lane asked.

"Not much. I woke up before you and was in time to see a group of people taken away by the guards, but that's about it."

"Taken away?"

"Yeah. Sometimes, someone appears on one of the beds. It takes them a while to open their eyes, and after that, the guards take them away. I'm pretty sure it's going to be our turn soon."

"What happened to those people?"

"You're asking the wrong person. I don't know anything except what I just told you."

It would make sense. Barnaby didn't look Egyptian, so maybe he truly knew nothing more. Lane tried to remember what he knew about the ancient Egyptian underworld, but unfortunately, it wasn't much. He'd tried not to pay too much attention to the gods because most of them were assholes. He kind of wished he had now, though, because he needed to know what was going on.

He got to his feet, careful of how he moved. He expected his body to be different, but he felt good. Actually, he felt better than he had in a long time. None of the aches that came with being alive were there anymore. His inner thighs didn't hurt from all the squats he'd been doing lately. His back was fine, too, and when he checked a cut on his finger, he saw it wasn't there anymore. He was as good as new.

Except he was dead.

A woman appeared between the guards. She was holding a tablet and started reading a list of names. Lane heard his and Barnaby's was right after him. More people stood from their beds, all of them looking confused. They glanced around as if they expected something to happen, but the only thing the woman said as she gestured at them to follow her was, "Come with me, please."

Her black hair was long, and she wore a white dress. The tablet was odd in her hand because of how modern it was, and Lane briefly wondered how they got any signal down here. He was dead, yet people in the underworld were able to use tablets. How did any of this make sense?

"Where are you taking us?" a man asked.

The woman paused and turned to look at him. "To the weighing ceremony."

Lane raked his brain, trying to remember what that was, but it didn't ring a bell. The man seemed to know what it was, because he stepped back and shook his head.

"I'm not going through that."

The woman arched a brow. "Aren't you? Well, you can't stay here forever, and going through the ceremony is the only way for you to make it to the next chapter of your life."

"I know what's going to happen if my heart is too heavy," the man protested.

The woman grinned, but it wasn't a nice smile. "Then, hopefully for you, your heart won't be. This is a *you* problem, though, not a *me* problem. I'm just doing my job, and if you don't follow me willingly, these gentlemen will drag you to the throne room." She gestured at the guards, and both of them took a step forward in unison.

The man who'd been protesting paled. His hands shook, but it was clear to everyone that he wouldn't have a choice. He'd have to follow the woman or be dragged, and Lane couldn't imagine that would be any more comfortable.

Lane leaned closer to Barnaby. His new friend was taller by a couple of inches, and his stomach was more padded than Lane's. It didn't take away from his cuteness, and Lane wondered if they'd have been friends if they'd still been alive. They probably would never have met, so it was useless to worry about that.

"Do you know what she was talking about?" he asked.

Barnaby moved closer. He opened his mouth, but before he could explain anything, one of the guards came closer. He gestured at them to follow the woman, and Lane obeyed. He wasn't about to start a scene when he didn't know what was happening. Besides, he was already dead. How much worse could it be?

He'd never see his family again. He could only imagine how much pain they would be in when they found out what had happened to him. It was ridiculous. He'd been stabbed because the guy had wanted his phone, and he hadn't moved quickly enough when handing it over. He wanted to find the guy and beat him up, and he hoped his attacker spend the rest of his life in jail. He would probably never find out.

They stepped out of the door and into a hallway. The walls were white here, too, but they were decorated in the ancient Egyptian style. Lane remembered that Egyptians told stories that way, so he tried to make sense of the art. Maybe it would help him understand what was about to happen to him and Barnaby.

A loud scream came from somewhere down the hallway. Everyone stopped moving. Lane and Barnaby looked at each other when it was clear no one wanted to keep going. The woman who was guiding them toward the scream didn't seem to care, though, almost as if she was used to this kind of noise.

Maybe she was. It couldn't be easy to work in the under-world.

"Follow me," she said again, her rhythm never faltering. "The ceremony doesn't take long, and once we know where you belong, you'll be sorted. This is the next step in your life after death and the most important."

Lane couldn't help but wonder if he and Barnaby were going to survive it.

Osiris sat on his throne, an elbow propped up on the armrest, his chin in his hand. Ammit finished eating her soul, snapping her teeth as she did so. She looked satisfied, which was understandable, but Osiris was bored.

Everything was always the same. As the god of the under-world, he had to preside over the daily weighing ceremonies. He'd lost count of how many he'd had to watch, and while in the beginning, he'd been intrigued and had felt like they were doing the right thing, by now, he'd seen too many humans being eaten by Ammit.

"The next group is here," his assistant murmured behind him.

Osiris didn't move. He didn't need to for the ceremony to continue. Edwin had everything in hand, and he gestured for the group to be let in.

As annoyed as Osiris was with his day and his work, he wouldn't be able to do it without Edwin. The man had been Osiris's assistant for close to two hundred years, and Osiris hoped he had no intention of ever retiring. It would be his right, especially after two hundred years of work, but Osiris considered him a friend and didn't want to lose him.

Edwin clicked his tongue at the sight of the group shuffling in. They all looked around, their expressions ranging from terrified to confused. Some of them had no idea what was about to happen, while others clearly knew, given their expressions.

Those were always the most interesting ones, and Osiris leaned forward. One of the men tried to step back, possibly to run, but the guards would have none of that. One of the guards stepped closer and pushed the man forward, and he stumbled away from the entrance and right into the middle of the room.

Ammit turned her head to look at him. That was when the others caught sight of her, and Osiris heard several people protest and even one sob. He could understand why. Ammit wasn't the cutest pet, but then, she wasn't a pet. She had a job to do, and she did it well, as some of the people she was about to judge knew.

Osiris looked at Thoth, who nodded and raised his tablet to signal he was ready. Osiris gestured at the guards to take the first man to the scale. The man tried to move away, but the guards wouldn't let him. Every single soul who ended up in the Egyptian underworld had to go through with this ceremony, and this man wouldn't be any different.

"Please," he begged. "I swear I didn't mean to hurt people."

That explained why he was so frightened. Osiris straightened on his throne, glaring at the man. "My only role is to watch the ceremony. I have no influence on what's about to happen or how much your heart weighs. The only thing that does is your behavior while you were alive."

Some of the people behind the first man started whispering to each other. Osiris sighed and turned his attention to them. He might as well explain what was about to happen. "You were sorted into the Egyptian underworld. That means your heart will be weighed on the scale in front of you." Osiris pointed at the feather on one side of the scale. "If your heart is as light as the feather, you'll be welcome in the underworld. If it's heavier, Ammit will eat it, and you'll cease to exist."

The whispers slowed down, then stopped. The newly dead stared at Osiris, most of them with wide eyes and in shock. Osiris looked at them, wondering how many would have light hearts and how many would end up as Ammit's dinner.

His gaze caught on one of the men standing at the back of the group. He was close to another man, but they didn't touch. The second man whispered something in the first man's ear, while the first man stared at Osiris instead of at Ammit or the scale like everyone else in the group.

The man's hair was short and blond, and while Osiris couldn't see his eyes from here, he felt as if the man was staring right through him. It was ridiculous, but it made him want to get off his throne and talk to the man.

Edwin cleared his throat. "Let's begin," he said, nodding at Thoth.

The guard pushed the man who'd been trying to get out of the ceremony closer to the scale.

Osiris heard the entire group suck in a breath almost as one as the man's heart appeared on the empty plate of the scale. For a few seconds, the scale stayed balanced. Then, the heart slowly moved down, clearly heavier than the feather.

Ammit licked her lips and took a step forward, and the man who'd just failed the ceremony tried to scramble back. The guard pushed him toward Ammit, and she snapped forward, grabbing the man's ankle. He screamed, but it didn't last long. Ammit was efficient, and with just a few bites, the man was gone, as was his heart, leaving the scale empty for the next person.

Osiris sat back on his throne. The rest of the group was terrified, but he barely paid attention to them. His focus was on the blond man, and when it was finally his time to go through with the ceremony, Osiris held his breath.

It had been a while since he'd had a lover. Dead souls were easier than having a relationship with another god, no matter how minor. With gods came headaches, and Osiris already had enough of those. There was nothing to suggest that this man would want Osiris if he made it through the ceremony, but if he did, maybe he'd agree to talk to Osiris, and they could take it from there.

Osiris leaned forward as the man stepped toward the scale. He didn't try to move back as most of the others had. Instead, he stood tall as he stared at Ammit, who licked her lips. It was an odd sight, considering her crocodile head, and Osiris understood why most of the dead souls feared her. It wasn't just the crocodile head, though. The front part of her body belonged to a lion, while the back part was that of a hippopotamus. She scared every soul who came in for the ceremony, but no matter her job or how she looked, she was sweet. Osiris doubted anyone would believe him, which was just as well. Ammit wasn't sweet with the souls who failed the test.

The man stood straight as his heart appeared on the scale. Osiris leaned forward, trying to see better. Edwin made an odd sound behind him, but Osiris ignored him. For a moment, everyone in the room was silent, like every time a new heart ended up on the scale.

The scale didn't move. Osiris relaxed, leaning back again. Whoever the man was, he'd been a good person when he was alive.

The guard ushered the man toward the back of the room, but the man paused to wait for his friend. It was good that his friend passed the test, too, and Osiris watched them disappear through the back door.

After that, the ceremony went back to being boring, and Osiris lost interest. He couldn't stop thinking about the blond man. Who was he? What had happened to him?

Osiris twisted in his seat to look at Edwin. "Do you have his name?"

Edwin didn't look surprised. "The blond one?"

"Yes."

Edwin nodded. "His name is Lane. He was mugged and killed."

Humans were ridiculous. "Let me know where he ends up."

"Taken an interest in a human, have you?" Thoth asked from Osiris's other side.

Osiris glared at him. "As if you never dated any of the souls who came through this room."

"I'm at work every day. Where else would I find someone to date?"

He wasn't wrong. Neither Thoth nor Osiris spent much time away from the underworld. In Osiris's case, it was because he wasn't supposed to. He was king of the underworld and had been since his brother had killed him. It would never change, and he didn't need it to.

But sometimes, it was a lonely job.

Lane tried to stay back, but someone pushed him forward, and he stumbled through the opening in the wall.

"What are you doing?" Barnaby asked from behind Lane. "We need to get out of that room."

"Why?"

"*Why?* Didn't you see the monster that ate the hearts?"

"You heard Osiris. She was doing her job and only ate people who deserve it."

But Lane couldn't deny it had been terrifying. He hadn't known what to think when he and Barnaby had stepped into the room and he'd seen the creature. Osiris had called her Ammit, but that didn't feel fierce enough for the mix of crocodile, lion, and hippopotamus she was. She wasn't much bigger than a dog, but the rows of teeth in her mouth had almost sent Lane running. He was glad he'd resisted the urge after seeing what had happened to the first guy who'd tried to refuse to go through the ceremony. He'd been forced to, and to no one's surprise, his heart had been heavy. From what Lane had gathered, that meant he hadn't been a good person when he was alive.

That was when Lane started panicking. What made a good person a good person? Did a heavy heart mean you'd killed someone or had been intentionally cruel, or was even the whitest of lies a problem? Because Lane had lied lots of times. Hell, the last time he'd done that was this morning, when he'd told his mother she looked good with her new haircut. She'd been distraught, and he'd been trying to reassure her, even though the hairdresser had given her a bowl cut.

But that lie hadn't been enough to make his heart too heavy. Lane had passed the test, as had Barnaby, and now the two of them and the others who'd passed were ushered away from the room. Lane tried to look back because he wanted one last glance at Osiris, but Barnaby pushed him. Lane stumbled before glaring at his new friend, but it was too late. They'd left the room, and Osiris was out of sight.

"Stop ogling the god of the underworld and walk," Barnaby whispered.

"I'm not ogling anyone."

"I have eyes, and I could see you doing it."

Lane glanced around, but the others were either too shocked or too busy looking around to pay attention to them.

"He's hot—all right?" Lane said.

Barnaby rolled his eyes. "Again, I have eyes. I saw that he was hot, but he's still the freaking god of the underworld. Besides, I find the green skin a bit freaky."

That had been a surprise. Lane hadn't expected Osiris himself to be there, and he hadn't expected the imposing figure the man made. It wasn't just the green skin like Barnaby had mentioned. It was the fact that even though Osiris had never stood up, it had been obvious he was way taller than Lane. It had been how his black hair framed his face and how his black eyes stared at Lane, almost feeling like a caress. Lane could have sworn he felt it against his skin, even though the god had stayed on his throne.

But Lane hadn't been able to look away. As soon as his heart had been deemed light enough and he'd been shuffled over to the side, he'd returned his attention to the god and continued staring until he and the others had been led out. The only reason he wanted to go back to that horrible room was to get another peek at Osiris.

Because Barnaby was right, and Lane *had* been ogling the god of the underworld.

"You have one last decision to make," the woman who'd guided Lane and the others out of the room in which they'd woken up said. She was still cool and behaved as if this was everyday business for her, and to be fair, it probably was. He wanted to ask her that and many more questions, but he wasn't sure it was a good idea.

"What decision?" a woman asked. She sounded wary, which Lane understood completely.

"You can either move on or stay down here in the underworld."

Lane had no idea what that meant. He wanted more information before making any kind of decision, so he kept his mouth shut and listened.

"If you decide to move on, that's it," the woman continued. "I don't know what it will be like for you because it's not my job, but you've already been deemed worthy of a place in the afterlife."

"Isn't this the afterlife?" Barnaby called out.

Thankfully, the woman didn't turn to them as she answered. Lane was pretty sure she could smite Barnaby with her gaze.

"Yes and no. This is the underworld, and it's on the same plane as the human world, the world you come from. Technically, you're not allowed to leave this place except to move on to the afterlife, but being here means you're close to your family and the people you left behind. You won't be able to see them, but we understand that many people want that reassurance, at least for a while. If you'd rather join your family members who have already passed in the afterlife, you're welcome to do that. If you decide to stay, you'll be assigned a job, like taking care of the palace or keeping an eye on the demons."

"Demons?" Barnaby squeaked.

"There's been an uptick in their numbers, but you don't have to worry. Osiris keeps us safe. We only need you to warn the guards if you see demons."

Lane nibbled on his lower lip. He'd known he wouldn't be able to see his family again, but the thought of being close to them was tempting. He didn't have anyone waiting for him in the afterlife, so that might be the best decision. "If we decide to stay, can we choose to go to the afterlife later on?" he asked.

The woman nodded. "You can always decide to go to the afterlife. You earned your place there, and it's where you belong, but we'd appreciate it if you decided to stay around for a bit longer and keep an eye on the demons. Osiris does what he can, but even he is only one person."

Other people asked more questions, but Lane didn't hear them. He was already thinking about what he'd do next.

"You're staying, aren't you?" Barnaby asked as he knocked their shoulders together.

"I think so. I don't have anyone in the afterlife, and I don't know if I'm ready to go there." Maybe when Lane's parents passed. He hoped it wouldn't be anytime soon, and he was ready to wait for years to come, but thinking about being here to welcome them warmed his heart. Of course, there was no way for him to know if they'd be sorted into this underworld, or if they were, whether they'd pass the ceremony. The thought that they might not almost made him panic, but he told himself that no one in his family had a bad heart. They were good people, just like he was.

"I don't have anyone there, either," Barnaby murmured.

Lane was glad his new friend was staying. All of this was confusing and overwhelming, and knowing he wouldn't face it alone was good. So he and Barnaby went through what came next together. When Barnaby squeezed Lane's hand, Lane didn't push him away. If anything, he was glad for the contact. Barnaby was his rock in an ocean of things going too fast and moving in ways he'd never expected, even though they barely knew each other.

The woman talked to every single one of them. When she was done explaining things and asking for details, she gave directions, either to go to the place where they'd be led to the afterlife or to their new home. When it was Lane and Barnaby's turn, Lane requested they live together. Thankfully, the woman seemed to think nothing of it.

"You can have suite number five hundred and sixty-six," she said, taking a note on her tablet. "Names?"

"Lane and Barnaby."

She nodded. "Welcome to the underworld, and thank you for staying and agreeing to help. Someone will show you to your suite."

That someone was a man wearing a white gown like the guards. Unlike them, he was all smiles and chatted as if this situation was perfectly normal. Lane supposed it was for him, but he was glad when the man finally gestured to a door with a number on it.

Five hundred and sixty-six.

Lane looked at Barnaby. "Looks like we're home."

He had no idea what was waiting for them behind the door or in this new life in general, but he was about to find out.

CHAPTER TWO

The underworld was strange. Lane was dead, yet he still wanted to eat and drink. He was dead, yet he still felt tired and needed to sleep.

What was the point of being dead if he still felt like he had when he was alive? He had no idea and didn't know if he should ask someone. Even if he decided to, who would he ask? Barnaby was the only person Lane saw every day. There were others like them who'd died and had decided to stick around, but Lane doubted they could give him the answers he was looking for. There were guards and servants, too, but they tended to stay away from the dead. Lane had tried starting a few conversations with them, but after a few attempts, he'd stopped because they either ignored him or got flustered.

He and Barnaby had been assigned a suite of rooms that were more luxurious than anything Lane had ever lived in. Even the house he'd grown up in with his parents hadn't been like this. It was beautiful, and while it didn't help him miss his parents any less, it helped to have a place to call home and to come back to once he and Barnaby were done working.

Well, it wasn't exactly work. The two of them were supposed to walk around in a specific area and keep an eye open for anything strange. Lane had almost pointed out that everything was strange to the man who'd explained it to him, but Barnaby had elbowed him, so he hadn't. He wasn't quite sure what they were looking for because *demons* was a vague description, but he supposed that anything out of the underworld-ordinary would be that. So far, everything had been normal, and the work was kind of boring, but from the whispers Lane had heard, it was an important job.

He pushed the rest of his sandwich into his mouth and leaned back against the couch to stare at the ceiling. It was white, just like seemingly every wall in the palace. A lot of them were decorated, and Lane had started imagining the lives of the people drawn on the walls. It was probably stupid, but it was a distraction, and the rest of his afterlife was kind of boring.

The door swung open, and Barnaby came in. Lane gestured at the platter of sandwiches on the table, and Barnaby made a beeline for it.

That was another thing Lane still wasn't used to. Things just *appeared* here in the underworld. Food appeared regularly, as well as toiletries and other things he and Barnaby needed. It was almost as if the palace was alive and could read their needs and thoughts. It gave Lane the creeps, but he closed his eyes and thought of ice cream, and when he opened them, a tub and spoon were on the table.

He grinned and snatched them up. "How do you think that works?" he asked Barnaby, who was stuffing his face.

"Magic. You'll never guess what I heard today."

Lane had learned that Barnaby was a gossiper almost as soon as they moved in together. Within a few hours, he'd known the names of all their neighbors and the guards who were in this area of the palace most often. He'd also had news about Osiris, but Lane had refused to listen to it. He didn't want to know how long it had been since Osiris had a lover or what the chances were that he'd take a dead soul to his bed.

Even though Lane wanted to jump up and wave his arms until Osiris chose him.

"The darkness," Barnaby said dramatically.

"That's what happens when you turn off the light."

Barnaby glared and waved his sandwich in Lane's face.

"Not that kind of darkness. The *Darkness*, the one with the big D."

"You can't just capitalize words." The ice cream was salted caramel, Lane's favorite flavor. He happily dug into it, not caring one bit now that he knew that since he was dead, his body wouldn't be able to change anymore. The few pounds he could have stood to lose would always be on his stomach, but he'd be able to eat as much ice cream as he wanted without gaining weight. As far as he was concerned, that was a massive win.

"You can when there's a giant snake god trapped in that darkness," Barnaby said. "He's a Bad Guy, and yes, that's capitalized, too. He's one of the big baddies who want to kill every single human being and create chaos."

That *was* interesting, and Lane sat up. "What did he do?"

"I don't have every detail, but his name is Apophis. He started a war with Ra or something like that, but he lost, and he's been trapped in the darkness ever since.

"Sounds kind of boring."

"He's a bad guy. No one cares that he's bored."

Lane certainly didn't, but being this close to such an evil being made him nervous. "Is he why they're having us poking around?"

"Kind of. From what I heard, he's been trying to get free ever since he was locked up there. He uses demons to do his bidding and stuff like that, and since he's dangerous, we need to make sure he doesn't go anywhere."

"And how are we supposed to do that? We're just us."

"Our job is to keep an eye on the demons. I'm sure Osiris will take care of Apophis if he has to."

He'd better, because Lane had no idea how to fight a god, let alone one who was a giant snake.

None of this sounded great, and Lane didn't want to get involved. From the glint in Barnaby's gaze, though, he knew he would be whether he liked it or not, so he wasn't surprised when, as soon as he was done eating, Barnaby jumped to his feet and grabbed his wrist.

"Come on. Let's go see the darkness," he said.

"You want me to go poking at the home of a giant evil snake?"

"We're not poking at anything. We're just watching it from afar."

"That sounds like a lie."

Barnaby laughed, and since Lane knew Barnaby would go with or without him, he followed his friend. He didn't particularly want to, but he wouldn't abandon Barnaby. He was Lane's only friend in the underworld, and Lane cared about him.

They had to walk farther from the palace than they had before. Lane didn't get tired anymore, which was weird but gave him the opportunity to look around. When he'd thought about the underworld, he'd imagined a lot of black rock, sand, and heat. He hadn't thought he'd end up in hell, but the underworld was, well, under, and that was what he'd expected.

He hadn't been entirely wrong. It was dark all the time. There was no sun here, so there were a lot of lamps. And there *was* sand and rocks and all of that.

But there were also weird flowers Lane had never seen anywhere else. There was wind, even though he didn't understand where it came from. It was warm but not too hot, and even when it got colder during the evening and at night, it was never too cold. It was a comfortable place to spend his afterlife until he decided he'd had enough and wanted to move on to whatever came next.

Barnaby sucked in a breath, catching Lane's attention. When Lane looked at him, it was to find him quiet and wide-eyed, so he turned to see what Barnaby was staring at.

It was a wall. Something told Lane it wasn't physical, but

he had no intention of poking at it to check if that was the case. It was entirely black and didn't seem to have an ending when Lane looked up. The black wall sucked all the light in front of it, making it look like an endless well that pulled Lane in.

Lane took a step back. Part of him wanted to go into the darkness, but another part told him to turn and run away as fast as he could. He wasn't about to move closer, and he grabbed Barnaby's hand, just in case his friend decided to be an idiot.

"I can believe something evil is in there," Barnaby croaked.

Lane could, too, and it worried him. He and Barnaby could always choose to move on to their eternal afterlife, but would they have the opportunity to do so? What would happen if the giant snake locked up in the darkness found its way out?

Osiris was bored again. It wasn't his fault that the ceremony was the same every time it happened, multiple times a day. There were so many more humans now than there had been in the past, meaning many more died every day. It was ceremony after ceremony, and Osiris wondered if there was anything he could do to make it faster. Could they mainline all of this process? There was only one Ammit, but surely, Osiris could find another way to banish the souls who didn't deserve the afterlife.

Edwin cleared his throat from his spot behind Osiris. Osiris rolled his eyes and twisted in his seat to glance at his assistant. "You can't tell me you're not bored," he whispered.

"I'm not admitting to anything. But I just got a message that Ra is here to see you."

Osiris blinked, sure he'd heard Edwin wrong. "I'm sorry. Can you repeat that?"

"Ra is here to see you. I had him put in your office. I hope it was the right decision."

"Of course." Osiris would have done the same. Where else were they supposed to put the sun god? Ra wasn't supposed to be in the underworld, so it was better for as few people to see him as possible.

Osiris got to his feet. Thoth, who'd been taking notes about the current ceremony, looked up, startled. Osiris had never understood why he had to be there to see the weighing of the hearts. He didn't do anything except watch. Thoth took notes about who passed and who didn't, and Ammit ate the hearts of the souls who deserved to vanish forever, but Osiris didn't have a task, which was one of the reasons he was bored.

"Please finish the ceremony," he told Thoth.

Thoth arched a brow. "Without you?"

"I have something to attend to, but I have faith in you."

Thoth was still staring, but he nodded. Osiris would have been lost without him and the many servants who made the ceremonies possible, but they could go on quite easily without him, and he wasn't ashamed to admit that. He was only here because he'd become the god of the underworld after his brother had killed him. He wasn't allowed to return to the palace where the other gods lived because his place was here now.

All because of Set. If Osiris ever saw him again, he'd strangle him, although he'd make sure not to kill him. He didn't want to have to spend the rest of eternity with him.

Osiris left the ceremony room in a hurry. He couldn't remember the last time he'd seen Ra, but if the sun god was here, it meant something important had happened. Osiris was separated from the other gods, so he didn't often hear the gossip, but considering the recent natural disasters in the human world and the new influx of demons, he could take a good guess.

Ra was here because of Apophis.

Osiris quickly made his way to his office. It wasn't far from the ceremony and the throne room, and it was the room he felt most comfortable in besides his suite. In his office, he could be himself. Only people he trusted were allowed in, and he seldom had visitors.

But today, he had one.

When he reached his office door, he sucked in a breath, straightened his back, and squared his shoulders. He might suspect why Ra was here, but he had no idea what Ra wanted. Probably his help, but Osiris could only keep an eye on Apophis from afar, nothing more.

He pushed open the door and stepped in. The first thing that caught his attention was the tall man standing by one of the chairs in front of the desk. Ra had always had an imposing presence, and that hadn't changed, even though he now wore human clothing. Gone was the white gown Osiris had last seen him in. Ra was wearing a suit, and he wore it well. The black of the fabric mirrored the black of Ra's hair and complemented his golden skin.

"Osiris," Ra said, inclining his head.

Osiris did the same. "Welcome."

Osiris's focus was pulled away from his who-knew-how-many-times great-grandfather. There was another man in the office, but Osiris didn't know him. From the power emanating from him, Osiris was pretty sure he was a god, but not an Egyptian one. He wore human clothing, too, but not a suit. He looked more comfortable in a flowing shirt and cotton pants. His long blond hair was braided and hung over one of his shoulders, and his green eyes were cautious, almost as if he expected not to be welcome.

So Osiris turned to him. "Welcome. I'm Osiris."

The man smiled. "Frey."

That didn't tell Osiris who Frey was, and he was tempted to ask, but he didn't have to because Ra cleared his throat.

"My partner," he explained.

Osiris stared. "As in . . ."

"As in, we're in love and live together in the human world. He's been by my side through everything that has happened lately, and I thought he needed to be here during this meeting."

Osiris was stunned, but not in a bad way. He was surprised that Ra, who'd been in isolation for thousands of years, had left the palace long enough to meet Frey and fall in love with him, and even more so to hear they lived in the human world.

"It's a pleasure to see both of you," he said. "Why don't you sit down? I can guess why you're here, and I believe we'll be more comfortable talking about it if we relax."

Ra wrinkled his nose. "I doubt I can ever be comfortable while talking about Apophis."

Osiris had been right, but he wasn't happy about that. He didn't *want* to be right when it came to Apophis.

He sat on the other side of the desk. He might as well get right to the point. "He's trying to get free, and he might succeed."

Ra didn't look happy. "We're aware. He has someone working for him, one of our minor gods."

"That would explain the recent influx of demons. More and more of them are appearing, so much so that I have to use dead souls to keep an eye on them."

"You're letting them fight?"

"No." It wasn't their job, and it never would be, but Osiris had to do something. He was only one god, and even the guards wouldn't be enough to kill all the demons appearing. "But they can monitor what's happening and report to me. We're trying to deal with the demons, and so far, we've managed, but it won't be long before there are too many of them." Osiris leaned forward. "You need to do something about Apophis. You're the only one who can."

Ra didn't scowl, but he didn't look happy." I'm aware, but

I wasn't alone the last time I defeated him. I need help."

"I'll do what I can from here." Osiris could leave his palace and the underworld, and there wasn't even a law or a rule that said he couldn't, but this was his place, and it had been so for much longer than he'd had a place in the palace where he and Ra both used to live.

"It's all I ask for. We're trying to find a solution and a way to keep Apophis where he is, but I won't deny that I'm afraid we won't be able to do it for long."

"The darkness is weakening." And Osiris could do nothing to change that. Ra might be able to do more, but he hadn't fought Apophis alone the first time, and there was nothing he could do on his own.

"We need to be ready for the fight that's coming." Ra sounded like he didn't think they could avoid it.

Unfortunately, Osiris thought he was right, and since Apophis was in the underworld, Osiris and his dead souls would be the first to pay for the time Apophis had been a prisoner.

Chapter Three

The underworld was strange, and not only because it looked nothing like the human world Lane was used to. It made him *feel* strange and like he wasn't entirely himself, and he supposed he wasn't. He'd gone through something he hadn't expected and that he couldn't fix. He was dead and had to leave his old life behind.

It made him feel flustered. He didn't like feeling aimless, and even though he and Barnaby had been given a job, it didn't feel like enough. What was Lane supposed to do beyond walking around and keeping an eye out? It wasn't enough, but he wasn't sure who to ask if there was anything else he could do or even if he should. Would Osiris get angry if he did? Or would the god understand what Lane was going through?

Lane had been asking around, so he knew a little bit more about what had happened to Osiris to make him the god of the underworld. He'd never meant to be this kind of god. He'd been alive before, and he'd no doubt had another job. Now, though, he was stuck here just like Lane was.

It couldn't be easy. It might have been thousands of years, but after Lane had watched Osiris hang around the palace, he'd come to realize he wasn't the only one bored here. As far as he could see, Osiris's only job was to be there when the ceremony happened and make sure the souls went where they should. Anyone would be bored with that task, especially after doing it for thousands of years.

Yet, Osiris wasn't complaining. He was doing what he was

supposed to do, and Lane should do the same, but he wasn't sure he could. The problem was that there was no way out unless he wanted to move on, which he wasn't ready for. The thought of not being here for his family when their time came made him panic, and he'd choose being weirded out and lost over that any day.

"What's going on?" Barnaby asked.

Lane was grateful for the distraction. "Nothing."

"Bullshit. You've been staring at the ground since we started walking. I thought I was your friend."

Barnaby could be a little dramatic sometimes, but Lane didn't know where he'd be if it weren't for him. Even more lost, no doubt. "You are."

"Your best friend?"

"In this realm, sure."

Barnaby flashed him a grin. "I'll take that. Now come on, why don't you tell your best friend what's going through your mind?"

Lane wasn't sure he wanted to talk about it. There was nothing Barnaby could do to make him get over the way he felt, and while Barnaby would probably understand, it wasn't his burden to carry. He might try to act as if he didn't have a care in the world and was more than happy to stick around the palace and even be dead, but sometimes, he lost himself in his thoughts, too.

That was when his smile vanished and when Lane could see the real Barnaby under it. It was when he could see the pain and terror, and that was enough for him to be sure that whatever had happened to Barnaby for him to die, it hadn't been pleasant.

Not that dying was ever pleasant, or at least, Lane didn't think so. His death certainly hadn't been, but then, he'd been stabbed. He didn't know what had happened to Barnaby, and he knew Barnaby wouldn't tell him even if he asked, so he hadn't. He didn't want to hurt his friend, and, more selfishly, he didn't want to lose him.

"I was just thinking about how strange all of this is," he explained, deciding to go with a half-truth. "One day, I was living my life, spending time with my family, working, and all of that, and the next, I'm here. Not only am I dead, but I now live in a palace in the underworld. I'm supposed to be keeping an eye on demons and that weird darkness. It's a lot to take in, and sometimes, it feels like maybe it's too much."

Barnaby hummed as he continued walking. "I get it," he said.

"Really? Because most of the time, you look happy to be here."

"That's because I am."

"Even though you're dead?"

"I always knew I'd die young. I was even looking forward to it, and I wasn't surprised when it happened. I understand where you're coming from, but I can't deny I'm fine here, and I wouldn't change anything even if I could."

Lane hesitated. "Were you sick?"

"No."

Lane was about to gently push to find out more about the circumstances of Barnaby's death when the ground started rumbling under his feet. He and Barnaby stopped walking and stared at each other, and Lane was pretty sure Barnaby's expression mirrored his. He looked shocked and a bit frantic, and his eyes had gone wide.

"What's that?" Barnaby asked as he grabbed Lane's hand.

"Maybe an earthquake?" It had never happened before, but Lane and Barnaby hadn't been here long. Maybe it was an everyday occurrence.

Except that couldn't be because it was the first time they felt something like this, and they'd been here several days.

"Are earthquakes a thing in the underworld?"

"I really hope so." Because if they weren't, it meant something else was happening, and Lane wasn't looking forward to finding out what that something was.

A long crack appeared in the ground in front of them. They jumped back, and Lane decided it was time to get back to the palace. He grabbed Barnaby's hand and pulled him in that direction, but Barnaby seemed frozen. He was staring at a spot behind Lane, and when Lane turned to look, he understood why.

Something was pulling itself out of the ground.

Lane's mouth went dry as he watched. Every instinct he had was screaming at him to run, but he couldn't seem to be able to. His feet were rooted to the ground, and his mind was trying to understand what was in front of him.

Black hands with fingers—so long that Lane couldn't understand what they were initially—grabbed the edges of the crack. The fingers were tipped with long claws, and they pulled the creature they belonged to out of the crack effortlessly.

Lane had never seen a demon before, but he was pretty sure that was what he was seeing.

Knowing that was enough to jolt him out of his shock. He was still holding Barnaby's hand and pulled hard enough for Barnaby to stumble. Barnaby turned his attention to Lane, but it was clear he wasn't entirely himself. Lane wasn't sure he'd be able to drag him to safety, but he was going to try. He wouldn't allow anyone to hurt either of them or to kill them for real.

"Come on," he said, tugging on Barnaby's hand as he started running.

Barnaby moved with him. Lane could have kissed him, but instead, he decided to keep his attention on the palace looming in the distance. They had to reach it to be safe.

"What are they?" Barnaby screamed.

Lane had only seen one of the creatures, and he didn't want to look back, but he felt he had to. When he did, it was to see more creatures emerging from the crack. Their skin was pitch black, and they had horns and red eyes. They were taller than Lane by a lot and looked deadly, even though they didn't carry weapons. The claws tipping their fingers would be enough to kill someone without even trying.

"Demons," he breathed out.

It was time for them to get out of there. They continued running, but Lane could hear the demons behind them catching up. They weren't going to make it.

Something in his stomach squirmed. He wasn't about to leave Barnaby behind, but he also wouldn't allow the demons to hurt him. That meant he'd have to convince Barnaby to go on without him while he tried to distract demons. He'd counted five when he looked back, and he was ready to face them all if it meant Barnaby could get to safety.

"You need to run to the palace," Lane panted.

"What about you? Why are you talking like you're not coming?" Barnaby yelled.

"Because I'm going to try to distract them. It'll give you time to get to the palace.

"I'm not leaving you!"

"We don't have a choice. It's not worth it for both of us to die."

"It is to me," Barnaby insisted, and Lane could see he wouldn't be able to change his friend's mind. Barnaby could be stubborn, always in the worst situations.

"Neither of you will have to die," a strong voice boomed.

Lane stumbled and almost fell on his face. He merely didn't because a strong hand caught his shoulder and hauled him up. He landed against the hard chest, and by the time he gathered himself and pushed back, Osiris was already striding away from him.

Lane stared. So far, he'd only seen Osiris as a bored king sitting on his throne. Right now, though, with his sword in his hand as he faced the demons, he looked like an avenging angel and every bit like the god he was.

Osiris had known what was happening as soon as he'd felt the ground shake under his feet. Usually, demons emerged alone or in small groups of two or three. They used existing cracks so no one noticed them and they could sneak away to the human realm. It was why Osiris had needed the dead souls to patrol the area and tell him if they saw demons. An influx of demons in the human realm could only spell trouble, which was something everyone was trying to avoid.

But this group of demons was massive. By the time Osiris reached them, he'd counted at least ten and had quit trying. He didn't care how many demons were there. He just cared that he and his guards would kill all of them.

With a yell, he raised his sword and launched himself into the fight. There hadn't always been so many demons emerging from the darkest parts of the underworld, but they'd always been a presence here. Osiris was used to fighting them, and he wasn't alone. His guards were well-trained, and even though there were many demons, it didn't take them long to dispatch the group.

Osiris was panting by the time they were done. His sword dripped black blood on the ground as he peered into the crack. It was hard to tell if it had caused the earthquake or the earthquake had caused it, but it didn't matter. The crack was there, an opening in the deepest part of the underworld that allowed demons through.

"We need to close this crack," he said to no one in particular.

He'd have to talk to Edwin about it. He was the one who

knew what to do in this kind of situation. He might not be a god, but he was better than most gods Osiris had met, and Osiris trusted him with his life.

"What should we do with the men?" one of the guards asked.

Osiris turned to see that Lane and his friend still stood there. Osiris had been surprised to find him and his friend running from the demons, and it had made him angry to see the fear on their faces. They were dead. They were supposed to be at peace, especially now that they'd passed the weighing ceremony. They weren't supposed to be running away from demons and in danger of disappearing forever.

He sighed. "I'll take care of it."

The guard nodded and turned his focus to the demons. They'd pushed the bodies back into the crack to give Edwin time to find a way to deal with all of this. In the meantime, Osiris had something to do, so he turned away from the crack and moved toward the two men.

They were about the same height and of a similar build, but Barnaby had wrapped his arms around Lane's waist and clung to him as if Lane was supposed to protect him. Osiris was intrigued by their relationship and told himself not to be jealous. He was nothing to either of them.

Yet.

"Did they hurt you?" he asked when he reached them.

Lane looked at Osiris. "Thank you. We would be dead again if it weren't for you."

Osiris found himself smiling. "I'm Osiris."

Lane arched a brow. "I already knew that. I mean, you're the god of the underworld, and I'm dead."

"It felt like the best way to introduce myself."

Barnaby giggled a little before slapping a hand over his mouth. He stared at Osiris with wide eyes, and Osiris smiled at him. He might not be as attracted to this man as he was to

Lane, but that didn't mean he didn't find him adorable.

"I'm Lane," Lane said. "And this is Barnaby."

Osiris already knew that, thanks to Edwin, but he went along with it. He didn't want to appear like a creep who'd been spying on the two, even though he just knew their names and how they'd died. "Well, Lane and Barnaby, why don't you allow me to walk you back to your rooms? I'm sure you can use some rest after what you've just gone through."

"I'm not sure I can walk," Barnaby said.

Osiris gestured at the nearest guard to come closer. The guard was there in a rush, looking like he was ready to carry Barnaby. When he tried, Barnaby squeaked and reeled back.

"What is he doing?" he asked Osiris.

"You need help to walk back to the palace."

"Help, yes, but I don't need to be carried." Barnaby let go of Lane. He appeared hesitant, but he took the guard's arm, and that was enough to help him relax. He sagged against the guard, who guided him toward the palace.

That left Osiris with Lane.

"Do you need help, too?" Osiris asked.

"I'm fine," Lane said as he started walking. "How did you know to come out here?"

"We felt the ground shaking. It usually means a new crack has opened and demons are pouring through it."

"So it's something that happens often?"

"It didn't until recently. It's been happening more often, though." And Osiris didn't think he could do anything to stop it. He'd been trying, but the cause was Apophis, which wasn't a problem Osiris could solve.

"And those are the demons we're supposed to keep an eye out for."

"You don't have to do it anymore if you don't feel up for it. But yes, these were some of the demons that have been coming out, thanks to the darkness." Osiris could mention

Apophis, but if Lane didn't know he was the cause, it would be better for him not to find out. He couldn't do anything about it, and he was already scared enough as it was.

"Do I want to know what's in the darkness?"

Osiris had no idea how to answer that. "Probably not." He wouldn't want to know if he had a choice.

"That's what I thought. Is Barnaby safe at the palace?"

"For now, we all are." But if Apophis came out of the darkness, no one would be safe, no matter where they lived. Osiris didn't want to freak Lane out even more , so he kept that to himself. Lane wasn't stupid, though, and even though he was scared, he probably could tell Osiris wasn't telling him everything. "I promise we're doing everything we can to ensure Apophis doesn't leave the darkness, but unfortunately, it might not be something we can stop."

"Maybe I should have taken your offer of moving on."

"You still can. There's nothing that says you need to stay, and you'd be safe if you did move on."

Osiris didn't know what it was like. He'd died, but his place was here in the underworld. He would never be allowed to move on because his presence was needed, but that didn't mean he hadn't wondered what it would be like. He wasn't sure why he didn't want Lane to go, but if Lane decided that was what was best for him, Osiris would grant it to him.

"I'm not going anywhere," Lane said.

"What about Barnaby?"

"You'd have to ask him, but I don't think he wants to go. He's scared now, but he'll feel better when we reach the palace."

Osiris found that hard to believe. "I can only imagine how frightened the two of you were." And probably still were.

"Well, it wasn't the most relaxing experience, but we're fine. It could have been so much worse."

It would have been if Osiris and the guards hadn't been there to intervene. Osiris needed to do something to stop these demons from coming out, but he didn't know what. He might be the god of the underworld, but his powers were limited. Apophis had come close to winning the last time he'd attacked, and several gods had allied to defeat him. They hadn't been able to kill him, but he'd been trapped.

He might not be for much longer.

But that wasn't something Osiris needed to think about right now. Now, he had to focus on Lane and Barnaby and make sure they were all right. After what they'd gone through, he wanted to thank them and reassure them, and he wasn't quite sure how to do that.

"Are the rooms you're staying in nice?" he asked as they finally reached the palace.

"Nicer than most of the places I've lived in. Why?"

"I could give you rooms closer to mine. They'd be bigger and more luxurious." And Lane and Barnaby would be close enough for Osiris to keep an eye on them.

Lane blinked. "Why would you do that?"

"I feel the need to do something for the two of you after what you've just come through."

"Well, you don't have to. We both decided to stick around, and we knew what was expected of us. It was scarier than we expected, but we'll be fine."

They would, for now, but Osiris couldn't help but wonder what would happen when Apophis finally came out of the darkness. He'd be bent on revenge and wouldn't hesitate to kill anyone who stood in his way, gods or humans. He'd never had any respect for life, and Osiris doubted that had changed.

He needed to protect Lane and Barnaby. He *would* protect them.

He just wasn't sure how he'd do that just yet.

Lane was right. By the time he and Barnaby reached the suite they shared, Barnaby was almost bouncing. He'd been very frightened earlier, but he seemed to be over it and to see what they'd gone through like yet another adventure.

"And did you see those claws?" he asked, turning back to Lane.

Lane was still walking next to Osiris, who, for some reason, seemed to have decided he needed to walk them to their suite. Lane wasn't about to protest, because it made him feel safe, even though they were in the palace.

Something about having Osiris close made Lane feel even more protected. He didn't want the sensation to stop, but he wasn't about to beg the god to stick around. Accepting his offer to move closer to his own rooms was tempting, though, and definitely something Barnaby and Lane should talk about. Barnaby would probably say yes before Lane could even explain the offer.

"I'm happy that both of you came out of this unhurt," Osiris slowly said as if he wasn't sure how to explain whatever he was about to say. "I'd like for you to stop going out to search for demons, though."

"Why? Isn't that why we agreed to stick around?" Barnaby sounded confused.

"It is, but it's become too dangerous. I'll find a solution. I refuse to endanger you or anyone else because of this. It's *my* job to keep you and the underworld safe, not yours."

"But we don't want to stop. Maybe we can stay closer to the palace or something, just in case, but I want to be useful. We both do, right, Lane?" Barnaby asked, turning.

Lane wanted to say no. He wanted to run away screaming, never come back, and, more importantly, never see one of those demons again. But Barnaby would do this whether Lane was with him or not, and Lane wasn't going to abandon him. Barnaby would end up kidnapped by demons or something similar if he were allowed to do this on his own, and that wasn't something Lane wanted to happen.

"We can continue working," he confirmed.

Osiris didn't look convinced. "It might be dangerous."

"Then maybe send a guard with every group out there," Barnaby suggested. "I mean, I don't know how many guards you have, so it might not be doable, but it's an idea. Or we could stick close to the palace so we can run back faster."

"I'll think about your suggestions," Osiris said, lightly bowing to Barnaby.

Barnaby beamed at him as if he'd been given him the sun. "Really?"

"Really. You're right when you say it's why you stayed back, and we need the help. As unwilling as I am to put anyone in danger, you've seen what you might encounter and can make your own decisions."

For some reason, that seemed to bring tears to Barnaby's eyes. He quickly ducked his head, but Lane had seen it. He didn't think Osiris had, and the tears were gone when Barnaby raised his head again.

Then Barnaby sucked in a breath. He was staring down the hallway.

When Lane looked, he understood why. He took a step back as Ammit, the heart-eating creature, ran toward them. He quickly looked around, wanting to find a weapon to protect both himself and Barnaby. He wanted to protect Osiris, too, but he was pretty sure the god could do that himself.

Lane turned to Osiris, wanting to ask what they should do. His eyes widened when Osiris crouched down, then opened his arms. The creature threw itself into Osiris's arms, and when it started licking Osiris's cheek, Lane had to wonder if maybe, he'd hit his head earlier.

That was the only way he could explain what he was seeing.

"Is it, like, your pet?" Barnaby asked.

Barnaby didn't appear afraid, which would make sense. He was the kind of person to poke at tigers because they were cute and wanted to cuddle with them. Maybe that was how he'd died. Maybe he'd tried to pet a bobcat or something like that, and he'd been mauled to death by what he'd call a kitty.

Osiris rose to his feet, Ammit in his arms, even though she was as big as a Labrador. "Not exactly. She's a goddess, but a different kind. You've seen what her job is."

"She's not going to eat me, right?" Barnaby asked.

He'd been hovering close, and Lane had to resist the urge to snap at him to step back.

"You've already gone through the ceremony. She knows you're worthy of being here, so no. She won't hurt you," Osiris reassured Barnaby.

"Can I pet her?"

Lane resisted the urge to groan. He'd known those words were coming. "Why would you want to pet her? Have you seen those teeth?"

Barnaby looked offended on Ammit's behalf. "Just because she has sharp teeth doesn't mean she's bad. Look at how happy she is."

She did appear happy in Osiris's arms, but then, wouldn't anyone? *Lane* would be happy if he were in Osiris's arms.

"You can," Osiris told Barnaby. "She isn't dangerous as long as your heart is light, and we already know it is."

Lane watched with wide eyes as Barnaby reached for Ammit. At least he was hesitant, which meant he understood it was dangerous, but that didn't last long. When Ammit tilted her head toward Barnaby as he started scratching it, Barnaby beamed, then moved closer.

If Lane wasn't careful, he'd find Barnaby and Ammit

cuddled on the couch of their suite next.

"She felt the earthquake and was probably worried," Osiris explained, looking fondly at Ammit and Barnaby.

"You think I could visit and play with her sometimes?"

Barnaby was going to get himself killed one day, or rather, he would have if he wasn't already dead. Lane wanted to remind him of the many teeth in Ammit's mouth, but he had to admit that while she looked odd considering the mix of animals that made up her body, she was perfectly happy to allow Barnaby to pet her and scratch under her chin. Anyone else would probably have lost their hand, but not Barnaby.

"You can visit my rooms and play with Ammit as often as you want," Osiris said warmly. "You, too, Lane. I'm sorry about what happened today. You should stay in the palace for the time being."

"We'll continue helping," Barnaby said. "Right?" He looked at Lane like he expected him to agree.

What was Lane supposed to say? He couldn't abandon Barnaby. He couldn't allow his friend to put himself in danger. What would happen the next time Barnaby stumbled on a bunch of demons? If Lane wasn't there to help, he might get himself killed, which wasn't something Lane wanted to consider.

He sighed. "Yeah. We'll help." He just hoped both of them would make it out in one piece.

CHAPTER FOUR

"More demons came out of the crack," Edwin explained, a grimace on his face. "We're working on closing it, but it'll take a bit longer. I've assigned several groups of guards to the area, and they should be able to keep the demons confined there, but the sooner we close it, the better."

Osiris nodded. "Is it still the only big crack we are dealing with?" There hadn't been another earthquake, so Osiris hoped there wasn't another crack.

"Correct," Edwin confirmed. "We've found several small ones, but they're easier to deal with. I've assigned guards there, too, just in case, but we have things under control."

He didn't add *for now*, but they both knew he should have. Eventually, things would get out of control, and there was nothing either of them could do to stop it. Ra was the only one who had a chance to stop Apophis, but he seemed as lost as Osiris felt. Eventually, though, he'd have to find a way to deal with this, because Apophis wouldn't stay in the darkness forever. If they didn't want the world to fall into pain and chaos, they needed to deal with the serpent soon. If he broke out, it would be too late.

"I want you to pull back the dead souls who have agreed to help us patrol the area," he told Edwin.

"All of them?"

"Except for the guards. If we don't, someone will get hurt, and I won't allow that to happen." Because Osiris was the god of the underworld, and these were his people. They were his to protect. They'd refused to move on and had agreed to help

Osiris, so this was the least he could do. It wasn't their job. It was his, and he had every intention of doing it.

If only he knew how.

"You think it's going to get worse," Edwin said, leaning back in his chair on the other side of Osiris's desk.

"The emergence of so many demons points to the fact that Apophis is breaking out. We need to stop him, but I don't know if there's a way for us to do so. When he was trapped, a group of gods had to work together to make that happen. It was a long time ago, and while things were difficult back then, I suspect they're even worse now. You know gods. You know how volatile we are and how easy it is for us to fight. I wouldn't be surprised if some of the gods who helped last time refuse to do so now. I'm pretty sure that's what Ra is currently busy with. He needs to gather as many gods as possible to help, but it's like herding cats."

"Cats with deadly powers and an immortal life," Edwin grumbled. "We all might die, though. Doesn't that include the gods?"

"It does, but I think that for many of them, it's easier to keep their heads in the sand and act as if nothing's happening. They don't want Apophis to be back, so they decided it just wasn't happening."

"They're going to get all of us killed."

He wasn't wrong. Even though Edwin, Osiris, and everyone else in the underworld were already dead, they still existed. That wouldn't be the case once Apophis was out. He'd probably come for Osiris first, since he was close and had kept him prisoner all these years. He wouldn't understand that Osiris had no hand in trapping him there. He'd just kept an eye on him and the darkness, reporting when something weird happened.

Right now, something weird was happening almost every day.

He rubbed his face. "All right. Keep the dead souls away from the darkness. Actually, try to keep them in the palace as much as possible. Tell them they're not expected to work anymore and make sure all of them are asked if they want to move on again. The more of them we manage to convince, the better." Because it would be fewer victims for Apophis.

"Does that include your new friend?" Edwin asked, a small smile curling his lips.

Osiris wasn't sure he had the energy to glare at him. "I don't know what you're talking about. I was worried about Lane *and* Barnaby," Osiris said, stressing the word so Edwin wouldn't think he only cared about Lane. "They almost died. They saw something their brain couldn't comprehend. It's not their job to be patrolling, and I don't want them to get hurt, but that goes for every dead soul who chooses to stay behind. I'm not sure you'll be able to convince those two to stop, though."

For some reason, Barnaby had sounded eager to continue patrolling. Osiris couldn't understand why after he and Lane had been attacked by demons, but he often didn't understand humans. He didn't have to in order to do his job, but he wondered if maybe he should try.

"I'll see what I can do," Edwin said.

There was nothing else either of them could do at the moment. They'd do their best and attempt to keep Apophis in the darkness. Then, they'd try to put him back into it when he broke out. However, many lives would be lost, and Osiris might not be there to help them in their transition anymore. Unfortunately, that wasn't something he could solve. It was Ra's job, and Osiris prayed he'd find a way to make it work.

"These rooms are massive! And have you seen the pool? There's a freaking pool in the underworld, and it's right outside our bedrooms," Barnaby said.

He was bouncing on his feet, looking like a little kid. Lane couldn't find it in him to berate his friend, especially because none of this was his fault. Lane should have known Osiris wouldn't listen to him. When the god had suggested moving him and Barnaby to the palace proper in his wing, Lane had said it wasn't necessary. Gods always did what they wanted, though, and in this case, Osiris wasn't any different. The day after the crack had appeared and the demons had almost attacked Lane and Barnaby, a bunch of servants had shown up. They'd explained they were moving Barnaby and Lane's things, and the only thing Lane had been able to do was to go along with it.

He wasn't sure he should be angry. He understood why Osiris wanted to give them this, but it truly wasn't necessary, and Lane didn't like feeling like he was being treated differently for no reason. He was a dead soul, just like the servants and the guards, and he didn't deserve special treatment.

Clearly, Barnaby didn't have a problem with it.

"I want to go swimming," he declared, already stripping.

Lane looked away. "It's not like we have anything better to do."

Barnaby stopped moving. "You're angry."

"Not at you."

"You can't be angry at a god," Barnaby said.

"I'm not angry."

"But that's not true. You don't want to be here." Barnaby hesitated. "I know the only reason you are is me. You don't want to leave me on my own because you're afraid something will happen to me. I don't want to hold you back, Lane. If you need to go, then go."

Lane strode toward his friend. He hadn't known what to think of Barnaby, and sometimes, he still didn't. His friend hadn't told him everything, but then, people seldom did. But

Barnaby was Lane's best friend, and Lane didn't know how he'd get through this if it weren't for him. He didn't want to contemplate being here alone, and he didn't want to hurt Barnaby.

"I don't need to go anywhere," he told Barnaby once he stood in front of him. "I don't regret my decision to stay until my family arrives. I'm just not sure what to think of the way Osiris is clearly favoring us. It doesn't feel right, but I don't know much about what should feel right. I haven't been dead long."

Barnaby crossed his arms over his chest. "You really don't know why he's doing this?"

"I'm assuming it's because he can. I thought he was different, but he's like every other god. He doesn't listen to what people want or say." Lane had never met another god, but he knew enough. *Everyone* knew enough to know it was better to stay away from the gods. Things never went well for the humans who decided to go and have a relationship with them.

"He's trying to protect us," Barnaby said, his voice soft. "I'm pretty sure he has a crush on you, which is the reason he put us here. But he's worried and scared and doesn't want anyone to get hurt. I think that seeing us being chased by those demons freaked him out. His job is to protect us, but he was almost too late and doesn't want that to happen again. You might think he's selfish, but I truly believe he's doing what he thinks is right."

So many things were wrong with what Barnaby said that Lane didn't know where to start. His mouth didn't seem to have a problem with that decision, though. "He doesn't have a crush on me."

"Doesn't he? Because every time you're in a room together, he can't stop looking at you. He's not going to hurt you. He's not that kind of god."

"How do you know what kind of god he is? We haven't

been here long, and it's not like we're spending much time with him." But Lane wanted to believe Barnaby. He wanted to believe Osiris was trying to help them, even though he was doing so by not listening to them.

"Look, I know how some people can be. I know what happens when people think they're better than you and don't listen to you and when they think they own you. That's not what Osiris is doing. He wants to keep us safe, and I'm sure that if it had been two different people who faced the demons, he would have offered them the same. He doesn't want any of the dead souls to get hurt. I wouldn't be surprised if he decided he didn't want us to patrol the area anymore."

Lane wanted to ask about the bit Barnaby had just confessed. Had someone thought they owned Barnaby? Was that why he was here?

But Barnaby wouldn't want to talk about it, and Lane didn't blame him. If something like that had happened to him, he wouldn't want to talk about it, especially if it had caused his death.

"You should go talk to him."

Lane blinked at Barnaby. "Talk to who?"

"Osiris. You think he's doing this because he's selfish and takes what he wants like the other gods, but I don't believe that. I'm sure you're wrong, and if you talk to him, you'll realize that."

"He's a god. He has better things to do than to go along with my needs."

"He put us in here. I'd say he decided to make us a priority." He paused and grinned. "Or you, anyway."

Lane rolled his eyes, but when Barnaby launched himself into the pool, he decided it was worth a try. He didn't want to think the worst of Osiris, but he was also afraid to allow himself to think that the god was doing this to protect him and Barnaby. The only way to know for sure would be to talk to him, so Lane left their new rooms and decided to look for him. Since they were in Osiris's private wing in the palace now, he should be fairly easy to find, but of course, that wasn't so. The palace was massive, and Lane got lost after turning a few corners.

Luckily for him—or maybe unluckily considering the reason for their presence—there were guards almost everywhere. He ended up asking one of them to show him to Osiris's office. He expected the guard to laugh in his face and tell him to fuck off, but instead, he nodded and gestured at Lane to follow him. Lane did, looking around as he tried to memorize the way they went.

Eventually, they stopped in front of a door. The guard bowed lightly, then walked away, leaving Lane on his own.

He bit his lower lip. He'd known what he wanted when he decided to come, but now, he had doubts. The god had better things to do than to listen to him rant about how his desires hadn't been listened to, but at the same time, he wanted answers. He supposed he should knock and see what happened, and that was what he did.

After a moment, the door opened, and a man appeared. Lane remembered seeing him at his ceremony and forced himself to smile.

"I'm looking for Osiris."

The man looked him up and down. "Well, you found his office."

"Isn't he here?"

"He is. I'm Edwin, his assistant."

"It's nice to meet you. Does he have time for me?"

Edwin stared for a moment before nodding. "Of course. Follow me."

Lane did, glancing around as he tried to make sense of what he was seeing. Maybe he should try to forget that Osiris was a god. He hadn't treated him and Barnaby like he was superior or anything like that, and Lane liked that. He supposed he'd see what happened once this conversation with Osiris was over.

Osiris was out of his chair as soon as Lane stepped into the office. He strode toward him, and once again, Lane was struck by how handsome the god was. He might have green skin, but it didn't take away from his beauty, which kind of flustered Lane because he wasn't used to thinking of people that way.

"Lane. Is everything all right?" Osiris asked.

"Yes. Barnaby is settling in." Lane narrowed his eyes. "I thought you'd agreed not to move us."

Osiris looked sheepish. "I apologize if I made you angry, but I wanted to be sure you were safe."

What was Lane supposed to say to that? How could he stay angry when Osiris had been trying to protect him and, more importantly, Barnaby?"

Lane sighed. "Fine. Let's say I'm not angry at you for doing that."

"That's all I ask for. Do you need anything in particular?"

"No. I'm sorry if I bothered you."

"You could never bother me. Why don't you come with me to the garden? We can walk and talk about how you're getting used to being in the underworld."

Lane was sure Osiris had better things to do than to take a walk with him, but he found himself nodding. He wanted to spend time with Osiris, even though he knew that way lay disaster.

He wasn't afraid of it.

CHAPTER FIVE

L ane woke up when his bed started moving under him. His
eyes snapped open, and he stared at the ceiling for just one
second. Then, he realized what was happening and tried to
get out of bed. The problem was that everything was shaking,
so he almost ended up falling on his face.

He grabbed the headboard, then the nightstand, and
pulled himself into a sitting position. The earthquake felt like
it would never end, and he didn't know what to do. Should
he stay here? He should probably go outside through the door
that opened in the garden, but he wouldn't leave Barnaby inside on his own.

He got to his feet. Holding himself against the wall, he
started to slowly make his way toward the door.

Then everything stopped.

Lane stayed where he was for a second, tense as if he expected another earthquake to start. Maybe he did, now that
he knew what the earthquakes meant. More demons were
climbing through a new crack in the ground, and somewhere
out there, there was a fight happening. The guards would
push the demons back, kill as many of them as they could,
and keep an eye on the crack, but unfortunately, there was
little else they could do.

This felt like a desperate situation, and Lane was pretty
sure it wasn't only a feeling.

"Lane?" Barnaby called out.

Forgetting his fears, Lane rushed toward the living area
they shared. Barnaby stood in the middle of the room with his

arms wrapped around himself. He was visibly terrified, and Lane pulled him into his arms for a second.

"We should go outside," Barnaby said.

"I'm pretty sure it's over."

Barnaby shook his head. "I don't want to risk it. I'm going to spend the rest of the night outside, and you should come with me. I don't want you to stay here and for something to happen to you."

"Grab your pillow and your blanket." They could sleep on the chairs by the pool. It would be more comfortable than sleeping on the ground, since Barnaby seemed bent on not staying inside the palace.

But Lane couldn't stop thinking about Osiris. Was he okay? There was no way he wouldn't have felt the earthquake, but Lane couldn't imagine what he was doing now. Had he gone out with the guards to kill the demons? He'd been there when the demons had attacked Lane and Barnaby, but that was a coincidence. Surely he wouldn't go out to fight, since he was a god.

"You're worried," Barnaby said when he came back with his pillow hugged to his chest.

"Well, I don't particularly like being woken up by an earthquake."

"We'll be fine outside."

Barnaby was right, but Lane needed to see Osiris. Barnaby had told Lane that Osiris had a crush on him, but he hadn't realized that Osiris wasn't the only one. Lane's crush on Osiris was just as strong, and he was worried.

"I think I'm going to go see if Osiris is okay," he told Barnaby.

Barnaby frowned. "He's a god. Of course he's okay."

"Well, I need to see it for myself. I'll be back as soon as I can. I'm sure he's busy, considering everything, so I won't be able to stay long."

Barnaby didn't look convinced. "Fine. I'll be outside by the pool. Maybe you can bring me back a snack?"

Barnaby sounded hopeful, and Lane couldn't help but smile. "I'll see what I can do. Try to get back to sleep."

"I doubt anyone in the palace is getting back to sleep tonight," Barnaby muttered as he made his way outside.

Lane stayed long enough to watch Barnaby settle on one of the chairs and wrap his blanket around his shoulders. Then he left their rooms, making his way toward Osiris's office. Unless Osiris was out, that was where he'd find him.

He was right. Edwin was sitting there when he walked into the first room where Edwin's desk was. His fingers were flying on his keyboard and he never looked up, but he gestured at Lane to go into Osiris's office. He wouldn't have if Osiris had been with someone in a meeting, so Lane didn't hesitate. He quickly knocked, then pushed the door open.

Osiris was behind his desk, a worried expression on his face. It smoothed out when he saw Lane—had he truly been worried? Lane had been, even though Osiris was a god. He wasn't sure he entirely believed that Osiris had a crush on him, but he sure seemed to care about him.

"I didn't want to wake you up in case you hadn't felt anything," Osiris explained as he got to his feet and walked around the desk. "But I was worried."

"How could I not feel that?" Lane asked. "I'm pretty sure everyone did. Barnaby decided to sleep outside by the pool for the rest of the night."

"The palace should be fine, but if he needs anything, make sure to let me know."

"He'll be okay. How are you?"

Osiris sighed and pinched the bridge of his nose. "I've been better. I've already sent guards out to find the crack and take care of the demons, but if this keeps happening, we're going to have a problem on our hands."

Lane thought they already did, but he wasn't rude or stupid enough to say so out loud. "You know how many demons came out this time?"

"Not yet." Osiris leaned back to grab his phone from the desk. "But I'm listening to the guards, so we'll know soon enough."

Lane had been amazed that technology worked in the underworld, but he didn't care about that now. He moved closer, listening to the voices coming from the phone. He was wearing his pajamas, which consisted of a pair of light pants and a tank top. Apparently Osiris hadn't had time to dress, either. He only wore a pair of pants that looked like they were made of silk, and Lane had to resist the urge to touch them to find out if they were. He was distracted by Osiris's naked chest, but he made sure not to touch as he moved even closer.

A warm hand touching his shoulder made him jerk back. He looked at Osiris with wide eyes, but the god didn't seem angry.

"I know you're worried, but I promise we're doing everything we can."

"I know." But Lane wondered what would happen when everything Osiris could do wouldn't be enough anymore. He knew the story now, and he'd been told how dangerous Apophis was. He was terrified of what would happen once the giant snake broke out of the darkness, but there was nothing he could do about it, and he hated feeling impotent.

"He's still in there," Osiris murmured, rubbing Lane's shoulder. "That's the first thing I checked once the earthquake was over. Apophis is still stuck."

Lane nodded, but while he was reassured, he knew it wasn't over. Apophis wanted out, and the fact that the earthquakes were becoming regular couldn't be good. Eventually, one last earthquake would break the darkness, and Apophis would come out. What would Osiris do then?

What would *Lane* do?

Osiris could tell Lane was frightened, and he didn't blame him. He'd been terrified when he'd woken up during the earthquake, sure that Apophis was breaking out and that soon, he'd come to kill him. He'd shaken himself and had taken charge because it was his job, but the worry was there. The darkness was still intact, and Apophis was still hidden deep inside of it, but how long would it take for him to find a crack? He was building an army of demons, and no matter how many of them the guards and Osiris killed, they kept coming.

Osiris didn't know what came next. He couldn't do anything to stop Apophis, no matter how much he wished he could. There was only one person who could act, and they weren't here.

Osiris eyed his phone. He could call Ra, but maybe it would be best for him to go to his great-grandfather. The problem was that he didn't know where to find him.

But he knew someone who would and would be happy to see him.

He smiled at himself and turned his attention back to Lane. "I need to visit the palace where the other gods live. Do you want to come with me?"

Lane blinked. "You want to take me to the palace where all your gods live?"

"Yes. I need to talk to someone."

"I'm human. I'm sure they don't want me around."

"They don't want me around, either. I don't care. What's happening is too important to let this keep us away."

"You're not wrong, but I don't want to be killed by a god who thinks I looked at him wrong."

"As long as you're with me, no one will touch you. I

promise you that."

Lane stared for a moment. "You know what? I believe you."

That was good, because Osiris wasn't lying. If anyone looked at Lane wrong, he'd make sure they knew what he thought of that, and if Lane was attacked, well, Osiris wasn't the god of the underworld for nothing.

He held out his hand after stuffing his phone into his pocket. Lane didn't move, and Osiris wondered if he'd changed his mind. Eventually, though, Lane put his hand in Osiris's, and Osiris pulled him closer.

"How does it work? Do we have to leave the palace?" Lane asked.

Osiris grinned. "Look around."

Lane sucked in a breath. "How?"

They weren't in the underworld palace anymore. Instead, they stood in front of a double set of doors Osiris remembered well from when he'd been younger. He'd spent a lot of time here, and it was one of the things he'd missed the most after he'd been sent to the underworld.

"Your Majesty," a voice came from behind Osiris.

Osiris rolled his eyes and turned to look at the guard. It had only taken a few seconds for them to find him. He was impressed. "Osiris."

The guard swallowed. "I'm sorry, but you can't be here."

"I'm not a king. I'm a god, and I belong here as much as the other gods."

"You're the god of the underworld. Please, let me walk you out."

Osiris glared. He'd known this wouldn't be easy. Many of the other gods didn't want him around. His place was in the underworld, and they'd been happy to wash their hands of him as soon as he'd been sent there. Maybe they wanted to forget the circumstances surrounding his death, or maybe they just didn't care about him. Whatever the reason, it didn't matter.

Osiris gently pushed Lane behind his back, just in case. He didn't think the guards would attack, but there were five of them facing him, and he wouldn't risk it. "I'm here to see Nu and, if possible, Ra. It's important."

"I understand, but you should go back to the underworld and contact them from there."

The guard wouldn't make this easy for Osiris. "I'll leave as soon as I see one of them. I know Ra doesn't live here, but I have a right to see Nu."

The guards looked at each other. Osiris was surprised they weren't shaking in their sandals. They were here to protect the gods, but they probably didn't have much work to do. The palace was only accessible to gods, so they were safe unless another pantheon decided to attack.

The guards clearly knew who Osiris was, so they'd probably been given orders when it came to him, but they also seemed wary of touching him or doing anything that might make him angry. They probably expected him to smite them or something like that.

He was tempted.

He grinned at them. "Eventually, you'll die, and when you do, I'll be your god. Do you really want to make me angry?"

The guard swallowed again and looked at the one standing next to him. "I understand, your majesty, but we were all given orders."

The door in front of them flung open. His smile widened when he found Nu standing there, their black hair all over the place, a scowl on their face.

"What's happening here?" they asked.

Their cat peeked out, saw the guards, and apparently decided it was none of his business. He disappeared into the room, and Osiris focused on Nu. "Hello," he said softly. "It's been a long time."

Nu stared for a moment. "Thousands of years. I'd say that calling that a long time is an understatement."

They stepped forward and grabbed Osiris, pulling him into their arms. Osiris went, closing his eyes at the familiar feeling. He might not have visited for thousands of years, but he remembered his life at the palace like it was yesterday. Nu had always been there for him, supporting him, and they'd been frantic after he'd been killed. He was surprised they hadn't killed his brother, but Nu seldom hurt people. They'd been disappointed, but they'd learned to live with Osiris being technically dead and stuck in the underworld.

"Well?" Nu asked as they leaned back. "What's going on? I'm glad to see you, but I can tell you didn't come because you missed me."

"Something's happened. Well, something is happening."

Nu sighed. "Apophis."

The guards started whispering to one another, but Osiris ignored them. "There was a massive earthquake tonight."

"Is he free?"

"No. He's still where he should be, and the demons the earthquake released are being taken care of. But this can't go on."

"I agree." Nu gestured at Osiris to come into their rooms. "Come on. I'll call Ra and ask him to come." They paused and looked at Lane, who was still standing behind Osiris with a hand on Osiris's back.

Osiris hesitated, wondering what Nu would think of him bringing a human to the palace. He should have told them who Lane was and why he was there, but he wasn't sure of the reason himself. He'd just known he didn't want to leave Lane behind in case something else happened. Telling himself that was the only reason Lane was here was a lie. He was worried about Barnaby, too, yet he hadn't wanted to bring him along. That was only Lane, and for a very good reason Osiris didn't want to think about at the moment.

"And who do we have here?" Nu asked, leaning closer.

Lane looked at Osiris with wide eyes. It was clear he didn't know what to say or do, so Osiris took the situation in hand. "This is Lane. He's one of my souls."

"He has to be important for you to bring him here."

"He is," Osiris confirmed.

Lane sucked in a breath.

Osiris was certain Lane wanted to ask what Osiris was talking about, but thankfully, he didn't. Osiris didn't want to do this in front of Nu and a bunch of guards. Besides, before he could explain why Lane was important, he probably should examine why he felt that way.

"Well, come on in, both of you," Nu said. "I'm delighted to meet another human."

Osiris blinked. "Another?"

Nu cackled. "You've missed so many things by not coming to visit. It's going to be fun to bring you up to date."

For some reason, Osiris was suddenly afraid.

When Lane had gone to bed yesterday, he hadn't expected to meet someone important to the Egyptian pantheon. He also hadn't expected the earthquake, and he didn't know how to deal with any of this. He was worried about keeping Barnaby safe, which was one of the reasons he'd agreed to come to this meeting. He needed to know what was happening.

He looked around as they walked into the room. He could hear the god talking to the guards in the hallway, and it sounded like the god was telling them to fuck off, albeit in a nicer way. "Who is this god?" Even though Lane had been doing his best to learn more about Osiris's pantheon, he didn't know every god. There were too many of them.

"Nu."

Lane's eyes widened. "You mean the god who created the entire pantheon?"

Osiris nodded. He was smiling softly, probably because Nu was just another god to him. Lane was freaking out, though.

"You couldn't tell me sooner?"

"Would it have changed anything?"

"I don't think so, but I would have been prepared. What am I supposed to do? How should I behave?" Should Lane bow or something?

"In any way you wish. They don't get offended by much."

Lane narrowed his eyes. "See. That's what I'm saying. They go by *they*?"

"Yes. That's the only thing you need to know. I promise they'll love you. You've seen how happy they are to have you here."

"I don't get how anyone can be happy, considering what's happening."

"I can't say I disagree, but you have to understand they're extremely old. They've lived through the first time Apophis was around, and I have no doubt they'll live through this time, too. They're worried, but it's not going to stop them from being nice and making friends with you."

Lane was supposed to be friends with Nu? How? His head hurt, and whatever meeting they were supposed to have hadn't even started. Lane needed to sit down.

He did so on a couch, and Osiris hovered next to him as if he was ready to run off in case Lane needed anything. Something touched Lane's legs, and he jerked back, looking down, half expecting a demon. There was no way for it to be a demon, considering where Lane was, but everything was so different up here. He'd never thought he'd visit this kind of place, and he had no idea what might happen.

But it was just a cat. A *mummified* cat, but a cat nonetheless, and when Lane reached for it, it rubbed his face against his fingers. It even purred, which was confusing as hell.

"The cat is dead," Lane said.

"He is," Osiris confirmed.

"Shouldn't he be in your palace, then? I mean, you're the god of the underworld and life after death."

"He should," Nu said as they came closer. "But I couldn't bear to let go of him after he died, and I think this is a fitting compromise."

Lane wasn't sure about that, but he didn't dare say it out loud. The last thing he wanted was to make Nu angry. He didn't know what kind of power they had and wasn't willing to find out on his own skin.

"I called Ra. He and Frey are coming," Nu explained as they sat on another couch. They turned their attention to Lane. "It'll take them a moment to arrive, so why don't you tell me about you?"

Lane stared. Surely, Nu didn't actually want to know about him. There were so many more interesting things to talk about.

Osiris's hand landed on Lane's shoulder and squeezed. "Lane recently died. He's still not used to the underworld and to the fact that he's not alive anymore."

Nu's expression was understanding, even though they'd never died as far as Lane knew. "I see. It's a pity that something like that happened to you, but I'm glad you found Osiris."

Lane nodded. "I'm glad I found him, too."

"You make a beautiful couple."

Lane gaped. "We're not together."

"Aren't you? Why not?"

"He's a god."

"And why should that be a problem? Unless you don't

want to date gods?"

Lane had no idea how to answer that question. Did he want to date gods? Hell, no. They came with too many complications. But did he want to date Osiris? He wasn't sure the answer to that question was the same. He liked Osiris, and Osiris didn't behave like a god. He had a lot of power, and he wasn't afraid to use it to keep Lane and Barnaby safe, but he'd never tried to use it against them. He hadn't forced them to do anything except move, and considering how happy Barnaby was, Lane didn't regret it.

"I didn't think it was allowed for humans to date gods," he said slowly.

"Who said that? I know plenty of gods who are dating humans. Look at Loki. He even had a child with his human."

Lane had no idea what to say to that. He knew who Loki was, but that was where his knowledge about the Norse god ended. He didn't want to find out more about him, either. Gods complicated things, and Loki was the king of complications.

The sound of someone quickly knocking on the door made them turn.

Lane was glad for the interruption. Nu was nice, but Lane didn't understand them or what they wanted, and he hated being in the spotlight. He'd rather talk about Apophis than himself and his relationship with Osiris.

The door opened, and a tall man appeared. He pulled another man in by the hand, then turned to glare at the hallway.

"How many times do I have to tell you that I don't care?" he asked. "Osiris is in our pantheon, and there's nothing that forbids him to be here."

"He's the god of the underworld," a woman said.

Lane couldn't see her, but he instantly disliked her. She wanted Osiris gone just because of what he was, which wasn't something he could change.

"And?"

"He doesn't belong here. He belongs in the underworld," the woman insisted.

"While I agree, there's nothing that says he can't visit. He belongs here as much as you do, so I'd appreciate it if you stopped this madness. He's a god, and he's doing everything he can to help with Apophis, something I can't say about you. Unless you want to sit in on this meeting?"

Lane would have paid to see the woman's expression, and he leaned forward to take a peek. Unfortunately, he couldn't see her from where he was, but the second man who'd entered winked at him. Lane stared, not knowing what to do. Since they were waiting for Ra, he was pretty sure the guy with the dark hair who was bickering with the woman outside was him. What about the blond who'd just winked at him, though?

"These are Ra and Frey," Osiris whispered. "Ra is the sun god, while Frey belongs to another pantheon. He's a Norse god."

"That's allowed, too?" Lane blurted out.

Nu chuckled. "We're gods. There is nothing that isn't allowed. Although I'll be the first to admit that most gods I know lead a boring life. Not Ra, though, at least not since he's met Frey." Their gaze moved from Lane to Osiris. "And clearly, not Osiris, either. I like this new thing of dating humans. Maybe I can find a human of my own."

Lane stared. He felt he'd been doing that a lot lately, but he didn't know what else to do. He had no idea why he was here beyond the fact that Osiris had been afraid there would be another earthquake and had been worried about him. His place wasn't here. He didn't belong surrounded by gods and had no idea what he was talking about when it came to Apophis.

But Osiris's hand was still on his shoulder, and that was enough for Lane to want to stay.

"Apophis can't be coming back," the woman said.

Ra stood up taller, which was impressive because he was already tall. "Keep telling yourself that. In the meantime, Osiris and I will find a solution."

He slammed the door in the woman's face, and Lane resisted the urge to clap. While his place wasn't here, he was glad he hadn't missed any of this. He'd have so many things to tell Barnaby when he went back. Barnaby would be jealous, but that wasn't the most important part.

The most important part was that Lane was with Osiris, supporting him in any way he could.

Osiris was impressed and touched. He hadn't expected Ra to stand up for him the way he had, mostly because no one ever stood up for him. The only one who ever had since Osiris became the god of the underworld was Nu, and they were smiling like a loon at the moment, clearly gleeful at Ra's burst of anger. Osiris didn't know who Ra had been talking to, but he didn't care. He didn't want anything to do with people who thought he didn't belong here just because he was the god of the underworld.

But they had something important to focus on, and that was what they needed to do.

Ra hovered by the door briefly before shaking himself and moving to the sitting area. Frey was with him, a small smile playing on his lips as he nodded at Osiris. They didn't know each other, but Osiris thought they'd get along once they had the opportunity to.

"Sorry about that," Ra said.

"You didn't do anything you have to apologize for," Osiris told him.

Ra grimaced. It was odd to see him behave more humanely. In the past, every time Osiris had seen him, he'd been stiff as a board. It wasn't because he thought he was better than everyone else, as far as Osiris knew, but he kept himself separated from humans and even other gods. That wasn't so anymore, and Osiris suspected Frey had a lot to do with that.

"No one here has anything to apologize for," Nu declared. "Now, why don't you sit down? Osiris is here for a reason, and it has to be important."

Everyone's attention turned to him. He still hovered next to Lane, but he quickly sat down. He didn't want to be too far away, so he settled on the armrest of the couch Lane was sitting on.

"There was a massive earthquake just half an hour ago," he explained. "The darkness is still intact, but this doesn't bode well. There's another crack, the biggest of all, and while the guards are managing to push back the demons crawling through it, eventually, something is going to break. There will be too many demons and not enough guards. They won't be able to do anything about it, and it'll be a disaster. And that's without even considering the fact that Apophis is trying to break through. If he does . . ." Osiris didn't have to finish that sentence for everyone in the room to know what would happen.

Frey cleared his throat. "Obviously, I don't know much about Apophis, but I believe it's time for us to start planning what we'll do if he breaks out."

"Fight," Osiris said. "It's the only thing we *can* do. The only alternative would be to let Apophis do what he wants, and that's not something I'm willing to compromise on. He needs to stay in the darkness, and if he comes out, he needs to go back into it."

"Why don't you explain what happened the first time the gods faced him?"

As Ra started doing that, Osiris leaned closer to Lane, who was tense and uncomfortable. Maybe it hadn't been a good idea to take him along, but Osiris hadn't had it in him to leave him back. He needed his eyes on Lane to reassure himself that the human was all right.

"You don't have to be so tense," he murmured. "They don't care that you're here."

Lane snorted softly. "I'm pretty sure they wonder what's going on and why I'm here."

"They know what's going on. There was an earthquake, and more demons came through the crack that was created."

Lane twisted in his seat to look at Osiris. "That's not what I was talking about, and you know it. They'll want to know why the human is here. They don't know anything about me."

"So? I don't know anything about Frey except that he and Ra are together, and I don't care that he's here. As far as I'm concerned, we need everyone we can gather to fight Apophis."

Lane glanced at the other three, but they were talking. They didn't care what he and Osiris were saying, and it seemed to help him relax. "We know why Frey is here. He and Ra are dating. Besides, he's a god. I'm neither a god nor your boyfriend, which means my presence here doesn't have an explanation. I'm surprised no one has asked what the fuck I'm doing here yet."

A quick knock on the door made Osiris look up. Before anyone could get up, the door swung open, and a tall man with dark hair stepped in. He opened his arms, grinning at the room. "Here I am, ready to save the day," he declared.

Osiris blinked at him while Frey groaned.

"Why are you here?" Frey asked.

The man pressed a hand over his heart. "Should I feel wounded by your tone? It doesn't sound like you're happy to see me."

"I texted him," Nu explained. "I thought we could use all the help we can find when it comes to Apophis. Loki is strong and powerful, and he has the ear of many gods, not just in his pantheon. Even if he himself cannot do anything to help, he might know someone who could, and we need that."

Osiris stared at the other god. He'd heard about Loki and even the fact that he regularly visited the palace. It had annoyed him because Loki wasn't even a god of their pantheon, yet he was more welcome than Osiris. He clearly felt at home here.

Osiris told himself to let it go. It wasn't Loki's fault that people reacted to his presence in the palace the way they did. It had started happening long before Loki was ever involved with Nu.

"And what do we have here?" Loki asked as he moved closer.

His gaze was on Lane, who appeared slightly panicked. He leaned closer to Osiris, and Osiris didn't hesitate to drape an arm around his shoulders.

He was the reason Lane was here. If Lane needed anything, even only reassurance, he'd give it to him.

Loki appeared delighted. "Are you another human partner?"

"This is Lane, one of my dead souls," Osiris said stiffly. It felt almost like Loki was making fun of Lane, and Osiris wouldn't tolerate that.

Loki cocked his head at Osiris. "Let me guess. The green skin is a dead giveaway." He snickered. "Nice pun if I do say so myself. You must be Osiris."

Osiris nodded. He didn't know what to make of Loki, and while he agreed with Nu that they needed as many gods as they could convince to be on their side, he wasn't sure this was a good idea. "I am."

"It's good to see another human. I left mine at home with our son, but I'll make sure he comes next time. He'll be happy to meet another human with whom he can complain about dating a god."

"You're dating a human?"

"The best human ever created."

Osiris was surprised to hear that. He only had to look in his own pantheon to find several cases of gods dating humans, but they were all minor gods. No one cared who they were dating because they weren't deemed important enough. Osiris didn't feel important, but he couldn't deny he was since he had the underworld under his control. But Loki was an entirely different thing. He was one of the most powerful gods in his pantheon. The fact that he was dating a human was stunning, and it made Osiris wonder if maybe, since no one cared about Loki dating a human, no one would care about him doing the same.

Except he wouldn't be dating a human, would he? Lane was a dead soul, and that made him different. He wasn't part of the human world anymore, which probably gave Osiris more leeway. It wouldn't be the first time he had a relationship with a dead soul, although he generally tended to avoid it because they could get jealous. Besides, he didn't know if he wanted to date Lane or if Lane wanted to date him. The circumstances around their meeting weren't great, and they needed to focus on Apophis first. The world might not be here in a few weeks or even sooner. It would be of no use to think about what could happen with Lane, so maybe Osiris should push it to the back of his mind.

But when he looked at Lane, he realized how hard it would be to do that. It didn't matter that the world might end soon. Osiris wanted to be with Lane when it happened.

And he hoped Lane would want the same.

CHAPTER SIX

Nothing had changed. Lane had hoped that the meeting between gods would bring a solution to the Apophis problem, but while they'd talked for what felt like hours, they still didn't know what to do beyond gathering more gods to fight the giant snake. Lane hated feeling powerless, and that was what he was right now.

He was human. Hell, he wasn't even that anymore. He was dead, and there was nothing he could do against Apophis.

He couldn't have felt more useless.

"I'll walk you back to your rooms," Osiris said when they reappeared in his office.

Lane wanted to ask how that worked, but he didn't dare. His mind was reeling with everything he'd heard tonight and all that had happened, and he needed some time to make sense of it before adding more knowledge.

So he nodded and allowed Osiris to guide him out of the office.

The palace was quiet, which was a surprise. Lane glanced around, expecting people running in panic, but there was no one. It was still the middle of the night, but he found it strange to think that anyone who'd been here during the earthquake would have gone back to sleep.

He doubted he'd be able to fall asleep again, at least tonight. His mind swirled, and he was trying to solve a problem he couldn't possibly start to make sense of. He knew too little about Apophis, and he had no power. Yet he hadn't felt excluded during the meeting, and when he'd asked questions or had offered suggestions, the gods surrounding him had listened to him. That had stunned him, but he'd liked it. Maybe not every single god was a dickhead, after all.

"How are you feeling?" Osiris asked.

Lane turned to look at him. Osiris's green skin looked soft under the gentle yellow lights cast by the lamps, and it made Lane want to touch him. He knew better than to do that, and he cherished having all his fingers attached to his hands, so he kept them to himself. Still, it was impossible not to wonder why Osiris had wanted to take Lane to meet his family and include him in the conversation about the Apophis problem when he was nothing more than a dead soul that Osiris had only known for a couple of weeks. It might feel like much longer, but it wasn't.

"I know you're unwilling to move on just yet," Osiris continued when Lane didn't answer his question. "But I could send you as far away from the darkness as possible. Maybe I could even talk to some of the other underworld gods and find you a place in their pantheon. You'd be safer there."

Lane blinked. "Isn't Apophis trying to destroy the entire world?"

"That's his goal, unless he's changed over the thousands of years he's been locked in the darkness, but I doubt it."

Lane nodded. "So even if I were to live in another underworld, he'd probably manage to get to me. He'd end up killing me anyway." Lane shook his head. "It's no use. I'd rather stay here where I already have a friend and you. I don't want to have to deal with a new god of the underworld or a new underworld. I'm fine where I am."

"I just wish I could do more for you. I'm worried something will happen to you."

"Something will happen whether I'm here or in another underworld. I'll be fine." Or at least, Lane hoped he would be. Given what was happening, though, he doubted anyone would be fine. It didn't matter if they were a dead soul or a god. Apophis wanted blood and revenge. If he got out, he'd get it.

"You're so much more than I expected any human to be," Osiris murmured.

Lane wasn't sure if he should be offended. "I might look brave, but I'm freaking out."

"No one blames you for feeling that way. I certainly don't."

"It's just all confusing, you know? A few weeks ago, I was living my normal life, only worried about bills and what I was going to eat for dinner that day. Then I died, and here I am, in the underworld, facing a kind of enemy I could only imagine facing before. It feels unreal and too real at the same time, and I don't think my brain can make sense of it."

"That's one of the reasons I offered to get you away. You could even take Barnaby along, since I know you're worried about him. This isn't your fight, Lane. You might get hurt even if you move to another underworld, but you'd be further away from Apophis, and it might give you a chance to make it out in one piece. I feel guilty having you here when I know how dangerous it is."

They reached Lane's door, and Lane stopped. He didn't know what to tell Osiris. The smartest thing to do would be to accept his offer, but he couldn't. "I'm staying," he said, looking up at Osiris. "I know it's not my fight, but eventually it's going to be everyone's fight. If Apophis gets out, he'll be a danger to the entire world, not just this place or your pantheon. I can't hide from that knowledge, and I don't want to. I'm pretty sure I'll be useless, but staying is better than hiding and praying everything will be all right. If there's anything at all I can do, then I want to do it."

Osiris stared at Lane, and Lane's breath hitched. Was Osiris about to kiss him? If he did, Lane wouldn't push him away. He'd been hesitant about doing anything with the god, especially considering who Osiris was, but he didn't care anymore. If they were going to die soon, he wanted to make the most out of this chance.

It might not be the brightest idea Lane would have or practical, but he didn't care. He was dead. He'd been killed for a handful of dollars in his wallet and his crappy phone. He'd had to leave his parents and his family behind, and he couldn't be sure he'd ever see them again. He wanted something good to happen, and if that something good was Osiris kissing him, then he'd kiss him back.

Osiris was impressed, but maybe he shouldn't be. He'd known humans were more resilient than one could expect by looking at them for a while. He'd been dealing with millions of humans since he'd become the god of the underworld, and he'd seen things and met people that had left him inspired and in awe.

Lane was one of those people. Anyone else would have taken Osiris's offer and run as far as possible from Apophis. Lane wasn't wrong when he said that Apophis would eventually destroy every single pantheon and the world itself if it got him what he wanted, but Lane could spend some time in peace, and if he was lucky, Apophis would never reach him. Instead, he was staying, and from the looks of it, he'd be fighting, even though he was human.

Osiris could only imagine what was going through Lane's mind as he decided to do this. The human would die instantly against Apophis, yet he was willing to try.

Osiris wouldn't allow Apophis to hurt Lane. He didn't care what he had to do to make sure that never happened. He'd do it. If he could, he'd destroy Apophis with his own bare hands.

Or at least he'd try, because he doubted anything he could do would hurt the serpent.

"You're strong," he whispered. "And brave, much more so than many of the gods I know."

Lane's cheeks turned pink, and he looked away. "I'm not doing anything weird. I've just decided to stay where I am, and I don't think I'm brave for that."

"I believe you are. Many of the gods who should be helping Ra still refuse to look reality in the face and accept that Apophis will probably break out of the darkness. They'd rather hide and continue their blissful life, and they don't realize that soon, they won't be able to do that. Even if Apophis doesn't kill them, he'll rule the world, and they'll have to bow to him. Things will change, which is exactly why they refuse to accept this is happening."

Lane wrinkled his nose. "Which is kind of ridiculous. I mean, it's not gonna change anything for them to accept that Apophis is coming back. They can even attempt to stop him, yet they don't want to."

"Gods are selfish. We're immortal and mostly separated from humans, and it's easier for us to focus on the golden life we live in our palaces and on fulfilling every want we might have."

"You're not like that."

Osiris was glad Lane had noticed that. "I'm not, but I wouldn't say I was never that way. Becoming the god of the underworld has changed me in many ways, and after spending so much time with humans, I hope I've become a better person. You only have a limited amount of time and make the most of it. I think that's what gods are missing. Time stretches in front of us without limits, bringing on a sort of apathy that not many gods know how to deal with. Mostly, they carry on with their lives without changing anything."

"But not all gods."

"Not all of them," Osiris agreed. "I've changed, and I can see how much Ra has, too. I'm pretty sure most of that is due to Frey, but I don't think the *why* matters. There's also Loki, who I would never have thought would have a human part-ner."

"And a son. Did you hear him when he explained he was the one who carried his kid? I didn't think that was possible, but I probably should have. I mean, he's a god."

Lane had sounded worried and tired before, but this con-versation seemed to energize him. He was excited, possibly because Loki had birthed his son and hadn't been shy about sharing the experience, or maybe to realize that he wouldn't be the only human in their little group. Whatever the reason, watching him smile, seeing the pink of his lips and the red of his cheeks, made Osiris want more. Normally, he'd have hes-itated because Lane was human, and, considering their situa-tion, it wasn't the brightest idea. He still wasn't sure he should be doing this, but he found that, at the moment, he didn't care.

He leaned forward. Lane's eyes widened, but he didn't move back, even when it became obvious that Osiris was about to kiss him. Osiris grinned at the thought that Lane wanted this as much as he did. He shouldn't be surprised. He'd been pretty sure the attraction he felt was mutual, but he'd been trying to give Lane time.

He also wasn't sure if starting something now, with Apophis looming in the distance, was the best idea, but maybe it was. They couldn't know what would happen in the future. If Apophis broke free, the apocalypse would be upon them, and they might lose everything. It would hurt to lose Lane, even more so if Osiris allowed himself to fall for him, but it would also give him something to fight for harder.

That was what he thought of when their lips met. He was done resisting the attraction between them. No matter how foolish it was to start something, he didn't care. He just wanted Lane and give him the best life he could, and he'd do everything he could to make that happen.

Lane's lips were soft. He didn't hesitate, didn't step back. Instead, he pressed closer and wrapped his arms around Osiris's neck. He opened his mouth, his tongue coming out to play.

And play they did.

Lane felt perfect in Osiris's arms, and Osiris never wanted this moment to end. He pressed Lane against the wall, ravishing his mouth, unable to stop himself from stroking Lane's back and sides. It made Lane shiver and groan, which in turn made Osiris grin.

Kissing Lane had been the best idea he'd had in a long time.

By the time they stopped kissing and Osiris pressed their foreheads together, they were both panting. "I'm not sure this is the right moment to start a relationship, but I won't deny it's what I want with you," he confessed.

Lane snorted. "Really? I would never have guessed." His voice softened. "But I think that maybe it's the best time to start a relationship. We don't know what will happen next. We just know that if Apophis breaks out, he'll try to destroy the world, and that will take any opportunity we have to be together. I'm glad we're able to do this now. It's now that we need happiness and something to fight for."

That was what Osiris had been thinking, and he was glad to find out Lane felt the same.

No matter what the future would be like or what Apophis did when he came out of the darkness, Osiris and Lane would face it together. Being together would give them strength, and hopefully, it would lead to victory.

And if it didn't, they would at least have had this.

Chapter Seven

"We lost several of the guards," Edwin said, his expression mirroring Osiris's feelings.

Even though the guards had already been dead, it was a hard hit. With this final death, they'd vanished from the world. They hadn't moved on. They were just gone, and Osiris would always shoulder that responsibility.

He should be doing more. He should be out there, fighting with the guards, keeping away the many demons spawning through the cracks that opened daily.

Edwin put his hands on his hips and glared. "Don't even think about it."

Osiris was angry. He almost snapped at his friend not to talk to him that way, but he wasn't that much of an asshole. "You have to see that I could do more if I was out there helping," he said.

"And you have to see what would happen if you were to die. Who would become the god of the underworld, then? What would happen to the palace and the dead souls who live here, and even more importantly, to the souls who come in every day?"

Osiris slumped back in his chair. He wanted to rage, to push off his computer and everything from his desk, but he couldn't give in to the anger. That was when bad decisions were made, and one wrong step in the situation with Apophis would be enough to start the end of the world.

"They'd be taken to other underworlds," he said through gritted teeth.

"Why do you always have an answer for everything?" Edwin asked. "Fine. What will happen if Apophis breaks out and destroys *all* the underworlds? Then what? What will happen to the humans dying? Because you know they won't stop dying, especially if Apophis is out there, running around with his demons. We can't afford to lose you."

"And I can't afford *not* to do anything!" Osiris yelled, immediately regretting it. He rubbed his face. "I apologize. I shouldn't be screaming at you."

Edwin sighed heavily and flopped back into his chair. "I yelled, too. We're frustrated and scared, and not being able to do anything isn't helping. We can't lose you, though. No one here can. Besides, it's not your job to fight Apophis. Ra should be doing more."

Osiris couldn't say he disagreed. Edwin hadn't been there during the last fight with Apophis, though. He hadn't seen how dangerous and complicated it had been and how they'd had to gather the powers of many gods to fight him. He hadn't seen how hurt and weak Ra had been after the fact. But Osiris *had* seen all of it, and he was desperate for something to do and a way to stop Apophis.

He reached for his phone. He needed help, and he wasn't ashamed of asking for it. He wasn't doing this to save himself. He was doing it to save his dead souls and the humans who would die today, tomorrow, and the days after that. Their place would be in the underworld, and Osiris needed to keep it safe for them.

He'd never loved his job. He hadn't wanted it, but it had been handed to him after he died. It took a lot to kill a god, but it was possible, as Osiris's brother had shown. When Osiris thought about it, he wanted to find Set and hit him, but something told him Ra would need Set to defeat Apophis this time around, too. Osiris couldn't afford to do anything stupid that would push his brother away.

No matter how many of Set's teeth he wanted to knock out.

"Who are you calling?" Edwin asked, sounding wary as Osiris lifted the phone to his ear.

"Ra. He needs to know what's going on."

"Just don't yell at him, all right? I doubt it would do any good."

"Right now, I don't care what would or wouldn't do any good. I need help before the underworld is destroyed."

Then Ra spoke. "What's happening in the underworld that you're talking about it being destroyed?"

Osiris sucked in a breath and told himself not to jump at Ra's throat. "What do you think is happening? More cracks open every day, and more demons come out of it. We lost countless guards we're never getting back. We condemned them to vanish forever." Osiris would make sure people remembered them and their sacrifice, but it didn't feel like enough. Nothing did right now.

"I'm sorry," Ra said.

"Instead of being sorry, do something. We need to stop Apophis. He's getting too strong, and with the darkness breaking and cracks letting out demons, it won't be long before he gets out."

"We've been thinking about reinforcing the darkness, but I don't have the kind of magic that would take," Ra explained. "We don't know if there's anything we can do even with magic, but it's worth a try and better than waiting to see what happens."

A small spark of hope lit in Osiris's chest. "What kind of magic are we talking about?"

"We don't know. Nu is looking into it, and I'm sure they'll have an answer soon."

Osiris deflated. They were still nowhere, and Apophis was gaining ground rapidly.

"In the meantime, we'll come down to the underworld and

help you and your guards," Ra added.

Osiris frowned. He'd just had this conversation with Edwin, and he didn't want to admit Edwin was right, so he avoided looking at him.

"You can't put yourself in danger that way," he told Ra. "You're the most powerful god we have, and we can't afford to lose you. Who will defeat Apophis if the demons hurt you?"

"They won't hurt me." Ra sounded convinced of that, and probably with good reason.

He was the strongest god Osiris knew, except for maybe Nu, but Nu didn't often show how much power they had. Osiris wouldn't be surprised to find them somewhere in the underworld battling demons, although the rest of the pantheon wouldn't view it nicely. Nu had never cared what the pantheon thought, though, which was good.

Osiris swallowed and looked at Edwin, who shook his head. He didn't want Osiris or any other god to put themselves in danger this way.

But they had to do something. Osiris couldn't abandon the guards to the demons, and while Nu was doing what they could by researching the magic needed to reinforce the darkness, everyone else was sitting on their thumbs. Fighting demons would help with that, and hopefully, by the time most of the demons roaming the underworld were gone, Nu would have found something.

"I'll be waiting for you," Osiris said.

"Let me make a few phone calls, and we'll come down."

They hung up, and Osiris got out of his seat before Edwin could start nagging. He raised a hand, stopping his friend, and ignored Edwin's glare. "I understand everything you've told me earlier, and I agree with it. But I can't sit back and do nothing. I need to go out there, and I will, but I hope that knowing I won't be alone will help you feel better about it."

"Not really," Edwin snapped. "You'll still be in danger, and I don't want anything to happen to you."

"Why should anything happen to you?" Lane asked from the office door.

Osiris groaned. As much as he wanted to see Lane, he didn't want Lane to ally with Edwin in this situation.

Edwin clearly knew it, because he rushed to explain. "Ra and some other gods are coming down to the underworld, and they and Osiris will be going out to fight demons." Edwin stared at Osiris as he explained, silently daring him to tell Lane that wasn't the truth.

Unfortunately, Osiris couldn't.

"Is it true?" Lane asked.

Osiris went to stand in front of him. "It is. I can't stand back and do nothing, especially with the many guards who are dying. They're putting their souls in danger and are losing them because they want to protect the underworld. It's my job, and I can't let them do this on their own."

For a moment, Lane stared. Then, to Osiris's surprise, he nodded. "I get it."

Osiris grinned at Edwin, who glared. He'd lost this fight, but Osiris had no doubt he'd win others. The bickering was part of their relationship, and Osiris knew Edwin had told Lane everything because he cared.

"But I'm coming with you," Lane continued.

The words froze Osiris to the floor. "You can't come. You're not a god, and you don't have powers."

"I'm not saying I want to fight the demons. I'm not an idiot, and I know I wouldn't win. I want to stay close by, though. I want to see what's happening."

Osiris wanted to bundle Lane into a thick blanket and hide him in his bedroom. He was tempted to do just that, but Lane would hate him if he tried. As fragile as Lane was as a human, he had a will of steel and knew what he wanted. He wouldn't back down, even if Osiris said no. He'd find a way to sneak out, and Osiris would be worried and lose focus.

"You can come," Osiris said. "But you're staying as far away as possible from the fight. You can watch, if that's what you want, and I can't forbid you to put yourself in danger, but I need to know you're safe if I don't want to be distracted."

Lane huffed. "That's what they always say in books."

"I'm sure they have a good reason to. I can't lose you, Lane. Please don't make me choose between staying here with you and going out there to help my people."

Lane stared for a moment before nodding. "Fine. I'll stay wherever you tell me to stay. But I'm coming."

Osiris forced himself to nod because he didn't have a choice. This was a war, and Lane seemed bent on fighting it right along with him.

When Lane had promised to stay as far away from the fight as possible, he hadn't thought it'd be this far. He could barely see the crack running through the ground from where he was. He scowled at Osiris, but Osiris didn't seem to care. He just stared at Lane until Lane stopped and sighed.

"I just want to help," Lane said.

"And you can do so from here."

"I can't even see what's going on."

"You don't need to see any more than this. I shouldn't have brought you along, and I don't know what the others will think. More importantly, I don't want you to get hurt. You're my responsibility, and after everything that's been happening, I'm not ready to lose another soul, especially not you."

Lane knew how tortured Osiris was over losing the guards, even though Osiris never talked about it. Like Lane, the guards were souls who'd decided to stay back. Now, the ones who'd died again were truly dead and didn't exist anymore, and Osiris felt responsible for that. Lane would, too, in his place, and while he wanted to say that the guards had chosen to stay back and fight, he didn't. It wouldn't change anything, and it wouldn't make Osiris feel any less guilty.

"Where's the party?" a voice Lane recognized said from behind them.

Osiris looked resigned. "This isn't a party," he told Loki. "We're here to kill demons."

Loki grinned. "That's what I said."

Loki looked in the distance, and his smile widened when he saw the crack. Demons were crawling through it, and the guards were killing them. There were more demons than guards, and the sight made Lane's heart beat faster.

Loki clapped Osiris's shoulder. "Come on, let's go."

"Why did Ra even call you?"

"Because we're friends."

Lane had a hard time believing that. He wanted to follow the two, but Osiris wouldn't let him, so he didn't even try. He watched as another two men walked past him, nodding at him as they did so. They looked curious, and Lane was curious about them, but now wasn't the time to ask questions or to introduce himself.

Then came Ra and Frey. Ra looked tense, but Frey always had a smile for Lane. Seeing them here, with Ra carrying a massive sword, made him wonder what Frey had been thinking. He could see the same questions in the way Ra glanced at him, as if he wondered what Lane was doing here. Lane couldn't say he disagreed. He wanted to be here for Osiris, but he hadn't thought it through. He was useless, but at least from here, he'd be able to see if anything happened. It would be better than staying back at the palace and wondering what was going on.

Or at least he hoped so.

To Lane's surprise, Nu was there, too. They grinned at him,

and instead of following the others toward demons, they stopped next to him. They wore a flowy pair of white pants and a shirt of the same color and looked out of place here, watching demons. They'd be even more out of place in a fight, and Lane wondered why they were here.

"Are you here to watch the show?" they asked.

"This isn't a show. People got hurt and will continue getting hurt until the demons stop coming through the cracks."

Nu's smile was soft. "I know. It can't be easy for you to wrap your mind around all of this, but everyone is doing everything they can. I'm here to talk to Osiris, and I might be able to help if they need me during the fight. It's better for me to stay away for now, though."

Lane wanted to ask why, but it was none of his business, and he didn't dare. He wasn't a god. He was just a human, even though Osiris liked him. It wasn't like they were together or anything like that. They hadn't talked about it after their first kiss, and Lane was afraid to ask. If he was only a fling for Osiris, he didn't want to know.

He turned his attention back to the fight. The gods had reached the demons, and Osiris had taken out his sword. He wasn't the only one, and Lane found himself squinting at the light coming from Ra's sword. He was the sun god, and the sword was proof of that. He also knew what he was doing. He threw himself into the fight wearing a suit, and Lane watched in awe as the gods got into the mix. One of the two men he hadn't recognized raised his hand, and a gust of wind took away several demons. Lane had never expected to see any god in action like this, and he couldn't look away.

He didn't know how long the fight lasted. Once more demons were killed, the guards started pushing their bodies into the crack. It felt like they had to use more than a dozen bodies, but eventually, the demons stopped coming. It wouldn't last long. They'd get rid of the bodies and start crawling through again, but the crack was safe for now.

Lane hesitated, knowing he'd put himself in danger if he did this and not caring one bit. The demons were gone, and unless one was hiding behind a rock or something, he couldn't see any more of them. He wanted to go to Osiris, and while he'd promised to stay away during the fight, it was over.

He started forward, going as quickly as he could. He was still far away when he noticed a demon creeping behind Osiris. The demon jerked forward as Osiris turned. The demon raked its claws along Osiris's chest. Osiris screamed, and Lane's heart stopped beating.

The other gods took care of the demon. In just a few seconds, he was in pieces on the ground, and Lane was running.

Where had the demon come from? There had been nowhere for it to hide that Lane could see, and with so many gods standing around, they should have seen it. They shouldn't have allowed Osiris to get hurt. Lane reached Osiris as Frey checked his chest. Frey made a surprised sound and stepped to the side, and Lane threw himself into Osiris's arms. Osiris wrapped his arms around Lane, and Lane remembered too late that Osiris was hurt. He jerked back and looked down at Osiris's chest, grimacing at the sight of blood dotting his shirt.

"I told you to stay away," Osiris gently scolded Lane.

"I told you not to get hurt. We both disobeyed, so we're even."

Osiris arched a brow. "Are we?"

"I was scared."

"I'm fine, and the demon is dead."

Lane carefully avoided looking at the ground. He'd already seen what dead demons looked like and could do without it. Instead, he rose on his tiptoes and kissed Osiris. He needed to feel him and reassure himself that Osiris was okay.

Then he remembered the many gods watching them. His cheeks heated and he stepped back, but Osiris didn't let him go. Instead, he looked at him with a gentle smile. "I'm fine," he promised. "This is just a scratch, so you don't have to worry about it. We're all fine."

Lane nodded. He wasn't sure he could look at the other gods after what he'd just done.

"It's good to see all of you in one piece," Nu said, having reached their group.

"I'm surprised to see you here. I didn't think you left your rooms anymore," Osiris said, lightly bowing at them.

"The only reason I haven't recently is that there's nothing out here for me. The world is boring."

"It was boring until recently," one of the two men Lane didn't know said. He poked at a piece of a demon on the ground with his foot, grimacing when his shoe got dirty with blood.

Nu ignored him. "I'm here to see Thoth."

That got everyone's attention, including Lane's. He knew Nu had been looking up the magic needed to keep the darkness sealed, and he'd been curious if they were here because of that. He thought that maybe they had the kind of magic necessary to do that, but he doubted it now. Why would they be asking to talk to Thoth?

Lane didn't know Thoth very well. He remembered him from his ceremony, and he'd seen him several times since then, but Thoth was always working, and he intimidated Lane a bit. He was so smart that Lane was afraid to say something stupid in front of him.

"What do you need from him?" Osiris asked.

"Well, he's the god of magic."

Everyone was silent for a moment. Lane wanted to ask why no one had thought about asking Thoth for a spell to keep the darkness sealed, but he was sure he was missing something.

"I'd forgotten that," Ra eventually said. "I remember him being the god of wisdom and writing and of the moon and a bunch of other things, but I'd forgotten the magic part."

Seriously? Ra had forgotten that Thoth was the god of magic and might be able to help? Sometimes, Lane wondered what would happen to these gods if they were human. They were lost even now that they were immortal and had powers, so they'd probably die a stupid death if they were human.

"Let's go, then," Loki said, sounding too excited.

Lane was tempted to stay back or disappear as soon as they were at the palace. He wanted to see this through, though.

It looked like he'd be visiting Thoth.

CHAPTER EIGHT

A knock on the door made Lane look up, but he wasn't sure he wanted to answer. He was bored, but considering everything happening at the moment, he'd rather be bored than surprised. The knock sounded urgent, so Lane probably didn't want to know what was happening.

Barnaby had no problems with that, though. He waltzed in from outside, where he'd been lying by the pool, and swung the door open. Lane went back to staring at the ceiling, telling himself that whatever was going on, he didn't want any part of it.

He was useless. To be fair, he wasn't the only useless person. Every single god working on the demon problem had to feel the way he did. They'd had hope when Nu had come to visit Thoth a few days ago, but Thoth hadn't been able to do anything for them. He was the god of magic, but that didn't mean he knew how to do everything related to magic. He'd promised to look into it, and as far as Lane had seen, he was doing just that. He'd seen Thoth around the palace a few times, and the god always had a book with him. He was trying hard to find a way to keep Apophis in the darkness, but everyone knew it might not be enough. It was disheartening, and when he thought about it, Lane wanted nothing more than to stay on the couch and stare at the ceiling.

"Lane?" Barnaby asked.

Lane looked up. Barnaby seemed hesitant, which wasn't like him. He gestured at the person on the other side of the door, and Lane saw it was one of the servants who worked around the palace.

It was weird. He wasn't used to having servants, and he'd been doing pretty much everything he could by himself, but that was limited to the rooms he shared with Barnaby. He couldn't clean the entire palace, which meant he had to leave that to the servants.

The woman was wringing her hands and looked almost frightened, which was alarming enough to get Lane to set up.

"What is it?" he asked.

"A group of people has just arrived, and I can't find Osiris," she explained. "I don't know what to do."

Lane frowned. "What group of people?" And why was she asking him?

He supposed that the fact that he and Osiris were dating wasn't a secret. He wasn't sure he'd call it dating, but they were *something*, and everyone at the palace knew. They didn't seem to care, which told Lane he wasn't the first dead soul Osiris was with. He didn't care about the others, though. He only cared about what was happening between him and Osiris. Unfortunately for both of them, it wasn't much. Osiris was running this way and that, meeting with other gods, doing his job during the ceremonies, and killing demons any second he could. Lane wished he could take some of those tasks from him, but he couldn't. The only thing he *could* do for Osiris was to stay away and give him the time and space he needed.

"They're gods," the servant whispered.

Osiris hadn't told Lane that others would be visiting, but it wasn't surprising. After talking to Thoth, they'd all said they'd come again soon. They wanted to help with the demons, but Lane had been skeptical. He shouldn't have been, because yesterday, Loki had. He'd found Osiris soon after arriving, and the two had gone out. Two gods fighting the demons were better than nothing.

"You should try finding Osiris again," Lane told the

woman.

"I'm just not sure what to do with the gods in the meantime."

Lane sighed. He was going to have to step in, wasn't he? "Why don't you tell me where they are? I'll take them to the dining room, and it would be great if you could bring some food. I don't know what Osiris is doing, but he's outside the palace, and until he's finished, eating something will be a good distraction."

The woman looked relieved that Lane was taking control. She nodded and bowed at him, then hurried down the hallway, leaving him behind. He stared at her for a moment, wondering what he'd gotten himself into once again.

"You're going to have lunch with a bunch of gods?" Barnaby asked.

"I don't know. To be honest, I have no idea what's happening."

"Looks like you invited the gods to stay for lunch."

"You want to come?" Barnaby would be a good distraction.

He looked horrified. "I don't want anything to do with any gods except for Osiris."

"They're not bad people."

"I never said they were, but it's not my place."

Lane didn't insist. He understood where Barnaby was coming from, and if it was up to him, he'd stay here in the rooms and leave the gods alone. Unfortunately, his relationship with Osiris seemed to mean that people looked to him to solve problems when he wasn't available, so Lane needed to take charge.

If only he knew what he was doing.

He left the room after making sure he didn't look like he'd been lying on the couch since this morning—which was what he'd been doing. He could hear the voices coming from the dining room before reaching it, and when he did, he sucked in a breath. He could do this. He'd spent time with these gods before, and they'd been nice to him. He was afraid about the reason they were here, but he couldn't just stay away.

He walked into the dining room. It looked like everyone was there, from Ra to Loki, to the two minor gods who'd been here to help the last time the gods had killed the demons. Lane had learned their names since then, and he nodded at Sed and Qebui when they noticed him.

"I'm afraid Osiris isn't available at the moment," Lane explained.

Loki beamed. "That's fine. We can wait for him." He flopped into one of the chairs and rubbed his stomach. "Is there anything to eat?"

"I asked the servants to bring something, so you won't have to wait for long. I already sent someone to see if they could find Osiris, so I hope he won't be long. He's working outside the palace at the moment."

"We can wait for him," Frey said with a smile.

He was Lane's favorite, and Lane wasn't afraid to admit that. Frey was gentle and always had a smile for everyone, but when it came to fighting the demons, he'd been fierce.

None of the gods present in the room were bad people. Lane had been surprised to realize that, but he couldn't deny it. Ra was incredibly stiff, but he melted when Frey was involved, and he was doing his best to find a way to prevent the apocalypse. Loki was always teasing and smiling but was serious when he needed to be. His jokes helped distract the others, which meant the tension wasn't as thick as it would have been if he hadn't been present.

Lane was relieved when the servants came in. They looked at him to guide them, so he quickly gestured for them to put the plates on the table. Thankfully, they'd gone with finger food, so they didn't have to sit around the table for a formal meal.

"Look at you," Loki said. "You're at home here, aren't you?"

"I've been living here for a while," Lane said stiffly. Not very long, but Loki didn't need to know that.

"But I don't see anyone else doing this. You died recently, yet you look like you belong."

"Sit down and eat," Lane ordered before he could think better of it.

Loki's smile widened and he obeyed, grabbing one of the plates from the stack and snagging a piece of bread from one of the baskets. "I like you," he told Lane.

Lane put his hands on his hips. "I don't know if I like you, but I suspect I'll find out soon enough." He might as well stop behaving as if Loki would smite him for looking at him wrong.

Loki's laughter was loud. Lane found himself smiling. Loki might be a god, but as far as Lane was concerned, he was one of the good ones.

And wasn't that surprising?

Osiris stood outside the dining room listening in. Edwin had found him while he'd been outside, checking the cracks closest to the palace to ensure they were safe. He'd been alarmed when he'd explained that a group of gods had arrived and wanted to talk to him, and even more so when he'd explained that instead of finding him, the servants had gone to Lane for help. Osiris hadn't known what to think about that, but knowing how Lane felt about most gods, he'd hurried inside to save him.

He shouldn't have worried. Lane had been tense and careful the previous times he'd met the gods, but he sounded more relaxed now, and he and Loki were teasing each other. Osiris didn't know Loki well, but it was clear that Lane was softening, and it was thanks to the Norse god. He was a good ally, something Osiris wouldn't have expected.

"What are you doing lurking out here?" Edwin asked in a whisper. "You can't leave Lane alone with the gods."

"He's fine." But Edwin was right. It wasn't Lane's job to entertain the gods, especially since Osiris was right there.

He walked into the room, leaving Edwin behind. Edwin was as wary of the other gods as Lane had been and always used the excuse that he had work to do to stay away. That was fine with Osiris. He wouldn't force Edwin or anyone else into doing anything they weren't comfortable with.

"There you are," Loki said, beaming at Osiris. He behaved as if the two of them were best friends when they'd only met a few times.

But Osiris found himself smiling back — how could he not? Loki's behavior was infectious. He seemed to find something good in every situation and didn't hesitate to step in and help, even people he didn't know. He hadn't had to come that day when Osiris had gone up to the palace to talk to Ra, yet he'd been there and had continued being here since then.

"I am," Osiris said, looking around the room. "But I don't know why you're here. Has something happened?" Being in the underworld meant Osiris was often out of the loop regarding the human realm. Even with technology, it wasn't easy to keep up.

"Not as far as I know," Loki said before stuffing a piece of bread into his mouth. "Ra thought we should have a meeting and talk, and while I'm not sure what else there is to say about our situation, I wasn't going to miss seeing you and your boyfriend."

"Who said anything about us being boyfriends?" Lane asked.

Loki winked at him. "You might not have had *the talk* yet, but you will. Osiris looks at you with little hearts in his eyes."

Osiris was pretty sure he didn't, but trying to change Loki's mind was useless. Besides, he did like Lane, probably more than he should.

It would be best if Lane moved to another underworld, or if he didn't want to go that far, to another part of this underworld, but every time Osiris suggested it, he refused. He kept saying he wasn't going anywhere, and while Osiris was glad he'd decided to stay, he was also terrified. He'd seen too many guards die over the past few days. He didn't want anything to happen to Lane, and he didn't know how to protect him except by keeping him in the palace.

"Has Thoth told you anything yet?" Ra asked.

As usual, he wore a suit. He'd only been wearing something different the first time Osiris had seen him recently, and Osiris wanted him to return to that. The sweater had looked more comfortable, and so had Ra. It was almost as if he used the suit as armor, but he didn't need one. Everyone around him was family, including Loki.

"No. He's been working, then disappearing into his suite to continue researching. The few times I've tried talking to him, he shooed me away and scolded me for bothering him."

"I don't want to rush him, but something needs to be done."

Osiris almost snorted. "I'm aware of that. He's going as fast as he can, and I don't think rushing him will help." But Ra was right. The darkness was thinning a little more every day, and the demons they didn't manage to kill gathered there. They poked and prodded at the darkness, trying to open a crack into it. Eventually, they would, even though Osiris had placed guards all along the darkness' edge. They kept the demons away, but the damn things were sneaky, and more guards were dying every day.

"Why don't you sit down and have something to eat?" Lane suggested.

Osiris was happy to obey. He took a seat next to Lane, grabbed one of the plates, and started filling it with the many foods that were spread out on the table. He liked what Lane had organized and was glad to have a moment to relax, even though it made him feel guilty. He should be out there, working, and not in here relaxing with his family.

But he'd been alone for so long, and spending time with these people reminded him of what he was fighting for. Usually, the gods kept him at arm's length. Even Iris and Horus, Osiris's ex-wife and his son, never visited. They'd stayed away since Osiris had been killed, and Osiris doubted that would change anytime soon.

He supposed it didn't need to change. He'd been fine on his own, but he was even better since Lane had entered his life, then, the other gods. It was odd to feel like someone finally cared, but despite the dire circumstances, Osiris wouldn't change this for anything in the world.

He had people now. He had friends, people who looked to him for solutions and who wanted to help.

"This is odd, isn't it?" Ra asked from Osiris's other side.

Osiris turned to him. "What do you mean?"

"I know you haven't isolated yourself because you wanted to, but rather that it was forced on you. It's not the same as when I retired because of what happened with Sekmet. I thought I was doing the right thing, and maybe I was, but when I came out of retirement, I never thought I could have all of this." He looked around the table, smiling softly.

It wasn't an expression Osiris was used to seeing on Ra's face. To be honest, he didn't know Ra very well, so he didn't know what kind of expression Ra usually had during family dinners.

But Osiris knew what Ra was talking about. "It is odd," Osiris confirmed. "But also incredible, and I'll do everything I can to protect it."

Ra nodded. "The same can be said for me. I found some-thing I never thought I'd have, and I'm not about to lose it. It's one of the reasons I wanted to be here today. I realize that most of you think there's nothing else to talk about because we still don't know what we'll do, but we need to organize in case Apophis manages to escape. What will we do then? How will we deal with him?"

Osiris remembered the last time Apophis had been free and hoped it wouldn't happen again. The serpent was cruel and bloodthirsty, and with Osiris being so close, he'd proba-bly be one of the first casualties.

But he wouldn't be facing Apophis alone. He had Ra and Lane and everyone else around the table. They were only a handful of people, and it wouldn't be enough to defeat Apophis, but maybe, it would be enough to keep him away until they found a solution.

That was all they needed. *Time.*

Osiris wasn't sure they'd get it, but he wouldn't stop any-one around the table from fighting. It didn't matter that it would probably cause their death. Osiris would do it happily if it meant protecting his family and the people he loved.

CHAPTER NINE

Lane was getting used to having gods around the palace. Initially, he'd been worried because he was only used to seeing Osiris, and sometimes Thoth. More and more, though, Osiris's family visited. It was almost as if they belonged here, and Lane wondered if maybe, they did feel that way.

It had started after the lunch they ate together. Lane had been nervous, but that feeling had vanished. Since then, Ra and Frey had visited several times. Every time they were here, they spent time outside with Osiris, getting rid of more demons. Loki was here almost every day, and he'd even brought his boyfriend and their son a few times. Sam was nice, but it was clear he'd been worried about his son's safety, so Lane didn't blame him for not coming more often. Loki was helping a lot, and Lane was glad to have him.

It wasn't just their small group anymore. Every so often, a new god or goddess appeared. They were visibly uncomfortable, but usually, Ra or Frey were there to help them. Osiris needed everyone to fight the demons, so Lane was glad to see that some gods in his pantheon were finally accepting the fact that even though he was the god of the underworld, it didn't make him any different from them. He might be dead, but he was still very much alive and doing his best to protect the world, including the various pantheons. It was only right that they came to help.

"Loki is here," a servant said from the open door of the library.

Lane had started spending a lot of time here. He couldn't

read half of the books in the room, but since he didn't have much to do, he was trying to help Thoth. It was probably useless, but it was better than sitting on his couch and staring at the ceiling every day, so Lane was grateful to have something to distract himself.

"Where is he?" he asked, getting to his feet.

"He went out."

So Loki was already hunting demons. That was good, yet at the same time, it was bad because they were so many demons that the gods who visited could barely take any time to rest. Osiris had been running himself ragged, and while Lane wanted to tell him to slow down, he didn't want to be patronizing. Osiris knew what he was doing and why he was doing it. He couldn't do anything different, and Lane would never ask him to.

"I saw him!" Barnaby said from behind the servant.

She stepped aside to let Barnaby into the library. He'd started wearing the same clothing as most of the people around the palace, which in this case, were loose pants and a shirt. His cheeks were red, and he looked like he'd met someone famous. Lane was pretty sure he was talking about Loki, though.

"Who did you see?"

"Loki. I didn't know if I should believe you when you said he'd come around, because he's a Norse god, but I saw him today. He was laughing as he ran out to attack demons."

That sounded like something Loki would do. "Do you want me to introduce you?"

Barnaby's eyes widened. "I can't think of anything worse. No, I don't want to talk to him. I'm fine staring at him from afar." He grinned. "Have you seen his ass in those leather pants he wears?"

Lane had to admit he had. He might be falling in love with Osiris, but that didn't mean he didn't have eyes.

"Do you think he's in danger?" Barnaby asked as he moved to the window to peer outside. "Should we send more guards? Or is Osiris out there?"

Lane went to stand next to him. Before, the demons had been far away from the palace, and it had been easy to forget what was happening out there. But with every earthquake, cracks appeared all over the underworld, and that included the palace. A crack had opened there a few nights ago, but thankfully, it had been small enough that Thoth could close it entirely. That was good, because it was right in the middle of the kitchen, and it would have been a disaster to have demons flow into the palace.

But there were other cracks and so many more demons. Lane felt as if they were never-ending, and he didn't know what would happen if things continued that way.

He glanced at Barnaby. His friend was staring outside, bouncing on the balls of his feet. Lane was worried about him, and even though he already knew Barnaby would say no, he asked, "Are you sure you don't want to leave?"

Barnaby turned to look at him with a frown. "Why would I want to leave?"

"Because it's not safe. You were here when the crack opened in the kitchen. What would have happened to you if demons had managed to sneak out? I don't like the thought of you being in danger."

Barnaby raised his chin. "Because you think I like the thought of you getting hurt?"

"Of course not, but that's different."

"Why? Because you're in love with Osiris? Or because you think I'm too weak to stay?"

"That's not what I think." Lane might not know what was in Barnaby's past, but the fact that he was still here proved his bravery. That didn't mean Lane wasn't terrified. "I don't want anything to happen to my best friend, that's all."

Barnaby's expression softened. "And I don't want anything to happen to *my* best friend. I'm not leaving you, and I know you won't leave Osiris behind, which means all three of us will be sticking around." He bit his lower lip. "But I can't deny I'm starting to worry. The thing in the kitchen freaked me out."

"That's why you should leave the underworld. We can find you a safe place somewhere else, and I promise I'll visit."

"No. I want to stay and help."

Lane shook his head. "I don't think there's anything either of us can do. Even the gods are lost when it comes to keeping Apophis in the darkness."

Barnaby huffed. "I don't like feeling like this. How about we focus on what we *can* do? All these gods need to eat, shower, and rest, right? I know they're going home to sleep, but maybe we could make sure that after a fight, they have a change of clothes and a room where they can wash up. And we should gather bandages and medical supplies. They might be gods, but they can get hurt and bleed, too."

That wasn't a bad idea. Lane understood the need to do something, but he'd believed there was nothing he and Barnaby could do. Barnaby had come up with something. It might not be a lot, but it would mean they could do their part, no matter how small it was. "We'll need to talk to Edwin."

Barnaby grinned. "I can do that."

Barnaby had no problems with Edwin, just with the gods coming and going around the palace. If he was going to work with them, even if it was only to make sure they were fed, he'd need to get over that. Maybe it would help distract both him and the gods, and everyone sorely needed that.

The end of the world might be coming, but there wasn't anything either of them could do about it except make things comfortable for everyone involved.

"I'm sorry," Osiris said, feeling like nothing he could say would make a difference.

It wasn't just a feeling. The wife of one of the guards who'd recently died was sobbing in front of him, and he couldn't do anything to help her feel better. Knowing that her husband wouldn't be sharing the afterlife with her was too much, and she cried harder.

He was gone because Osiris hadn't been able to protect him.

She hadn't come alone, and the woman she'd brought along wrapped an arm around her shoulders. She nodded at Osiris, then guided the sobbing wife out of Osiris's office. Osiris waited until they were gone and the door was closed to flop into his chair. He rubbed his face, wondering how many of these conversations he'd have in the future. As long as Apophis was causing so many demons to come out, probably countless ones. Things would change once Apophis was out of the darkness, and not for the better. That wasn't something Osiris could afford to think about at the moment, though.

A quiet knock on the door made him groan. It was probably Edwin, but Osiris didn't want to see anyone at the moment. He just wanted to be in his chair, mope, and try to forget what was happening out there. Apophis wasn't going anywhere, and he'd be a danger even after Osiris was done moping.

The door opened, and Edwin peeked in. He nodded when he saw Osiris was alone and walked into the room, closing the door behind himself.

"You need to take time off."

Osiris blinked. "That's not what I expected from you."

Edwin snorted. "Normally, I wouldn't suggest this, but we've all been running on fumes. You, especially, have been busier than I ever saw you, and it's not good, even though you're a god. If you don't rest, something is going to break, and it'll probably happen during the worst time for it. I know you want to be out there helping your guards and keeping everyone safe, but it won't do us any good if you're not at your strongest when Apophis breaks out."

More and more, they'd started talking about Apophis as if it was a given that he'd break through the darkness, eventually. Osiris felt it was, no matter how little he liked it. He didn't want to have to face Apophis, but he couldn't hide from reality. He couldn't even try to when so many of his people were dying every day.

He was doing what he could, going out there and fighting, usually with the help of other gods. They were coming every day now, some of them staying for the night. It made Osiris feel less alone as he faced this mess, but it also worried him because the fact that so many gods couldn't do anything about Apophis made him wonder what they'd do once he was out.

Edwin sat on one of the chairs in front of the desk and leaned forward. "I know you don't want to take time off and that you feel guilty, but it's important. We'll need you when Apophis breaks out, which means you must be all right then. I'm not saying you need to go to the beach for two weeks, but maybe you could spend time with Lane."

Osiris grinned. "You're just playing matchmaker."

"I don't need to play matchmaker when the two of you are already making puppy eyes at each other. You haven't been spending a lot of time together, though, but you should. Don't let Apophis win."

The smile vanished from Osiris's face. "He will, eventually."

"Then maybe you should make the most of the time you have now. We don't know what will happen tomorrow, the day after that, or next week. We can only work with what we *do* know, and from what I can see, you care about Lane and he cares about you. He's been giving you all the space you need, and I'm sure he understands, but it's not fair to string him along."

"I'm not stringing him along."

"You're right. Those weren't the right words. But everyone needs rest, and everyone needs love. You have a chance at it, and while I know you believe it won't last for long because Apophis will break out, I think that's exactly why you need to take advantage of the time you have."

He wasn't wrong. There was no way for anyone to know what would happen once Apophis broke out of the darkness, but it wouldn't be good. Osiris and Lane wouldn't have time to be together while fighting Apophis and his demons and trying to survive.

Or maybe they would. Power was important, but so was love. Love was the reason people fought back and survived. Osiris hated putting Lane in danger, but Lane had made his decision, and deep inside, Osiris was glad he wouldn't leave. He needed Lane here—needed to know that whatever happened, he wouldn't have to face it alone. It might make him a shitty god, but he wasn't ashamed of needing Lane and wanting to be with him. With everything happening, they hadn't had nearly enough time, and maybe it was time to fix that.

"You know, I think you're right," Osiris said as he looked at Edwin. "Lane and I need time alone."

Edwin nodded and looked down at the tablet he was holding. "I've already organized for the kitchen to get a basket ready with food. You can't go far from the palace, but I got everything ready on the balcony in your bedroom."

Osiris laughed. He should have known Edwin had already thought of everything. He wished he'd had the opportunity to organize this date, but this was better than anything he would have come up with. His mind was always on fighting and demons, and today wasn't any different. But Lane deserved to be spoiled, and apparently, Edwin thought a picnic would be perfect for that.

Osiris got to his feet and walked around the desk. Edwin looked nervous, but he relaxed when Osiris leaned down to hug him. He pressed a kiss against the top of Edwin's head, once again wondering what he'd done to deserve such a good friend. It would have been so easy for Edwin to leave, especially now that Apophis was a nightmare they couldn't ignore anymore. Instead, he was here, helping Osiris in any way he could.

"Thank you," Osiris told him.

"You don't need to thank me." Edwin's voice sounded gruff. "I'm doing it for myself. The more relaxed and strong you are when Apophis comes out, the better you'll be able to protect me. Now go out there and find your man. Try to forget about everything that's not you and him for the night. All of these problems will still be here tomorrow. There's no escaping them, but you can take a break."

Osiris hadn't considered taking a break until Edwin had suggested it, but now, he couldn't think about anything else. He left Edwin in the office and rushed to Lane, wondering where he'd find him. Lane had started spending most of his time in the library, so that was where Osiris headed.

In his own way, Lane was trying to help. There wasn't much he could do, and he never missed a chance to grumble about that, but he'd decided to read the books he could understand in the library. He was trying to help Thoth, and while it was touching, Osiris doubted anyone could. This was something only the god of magic could do, but it was good for Lane to have something to focus on that wasn't what would happen when Apophis escaped.

Sure enough, when Osiris walked into the library, he found Lane there. He was surprised to see that Barnaby was with him and that instead of reading, they were talking. They both looked up when they heard him and smiled, but Osiris only had eyes for Lane.

It might sound ridiculous because they hadn't known each other long, but he missed Lane. They still hadn't talked about what they wanted and what they were to each other. They hadn't had the opportunity to do so, and maybe it was pointless if they were all going to die once Apophis escaped, but maybe they didn't need to talk about what they were. They just needed time together to enjoy each other's company, and thanks to Edwin, they had it.

"Are you busy?" Osiris asked.

Lane and Barnaby looked at each other. Barnaby shrugged, and Lane turned his attention back to Osiris. "Not really. We were working, but I can come with you if you need me."

"I do need you, and for the rest of the night."

Lane's cheeks flushed. "I'm not sure that sounded the way you wanted it to sound, but fine. Barnaby, you'll be okay with all of this?"

"I'm not an idiot. I have everything under control, so go with your man," Barnaby said, pushing Lane toward Osiris.

Osiris wanted to ask what they were talking about, but he kept that question to himself for now. He held a hand out, and Lane took it.

It was all Osiris needed.

Lane hadn't expected a date, especially not in the middle of the disaster that was his life at the moment. He'd accepted that his relationship with Osiris had started at the worst moment possible, and it had given him pause. He'd gotten over those doubts and had decided that if he only had a few weeks or months left before Apophis killed him and everyone else around him, he'd make the most of it. That was why he was all in with Osiris.

The problem was time. Osiris was busy, going from his necessary presence during the weighing ceremonies to the patrols he went on with the guards to the hunting of demons when they appeared after every earthquake. Lane had stuck to the palace, and there wasn't much he could do, but he'd been trying to make everyone's lives easier, including Osiris.

It felt a bit silly for both of them to take time off, considering what was happening outside the palace, but Lane needed Osiris to survive whatever would come next. That meant he needed something to return to and to be rested, and while rest probably wasn't what Osiris had in mind for their date, Lane would make sure the god got a good night's sleep.

"Edwin organized everything," Osiris explained. "I know I should have, but—"

"No time. I'm aware of the circumstances, so you don't have to apologize. I'm happy to have time with you, and I don't much care about how it happens or who organizes it." It wasn't a lie. Lane just wanted time with Osiris.

Osiris squeezed Lane's hand. "I feel the same."

And in the end, that was all that mattered.

Lane wondered what they'd find when they reached Osiris suite. He'd been in there several times, so he didn't bother looking around. His attention was on the balcony right away, and he smiled at the sight of the many pillows and blankets deposited on the floor. They were placed so that whoever sat there looked out at the desert surrounding the palace. It was beautiful in its way, reminding Lane of the world he'd left behind when he died. He'd never get it back, but the underworld wasn't that bad.

Giant evil snake notwithstanding.

"Why don't you go sit down?" Osiris suggested. "I'll be right there."

Lane nodded and obeyed. There was a basket next to the

nest, and he didn't think Osiris would mind if he opened it. He smiled when he saw the many finger foods packed into it and made a mental note to thank Edwin the next time he saw him.

Then he found the lube, and he wasn't sure if he should thank Edwin for that, too.

"That's not what I expected to find you with," Osiris said from behind Lane.

Lane flushed, but he didn't hide the lube. It was too late, since Osiris had seen it. "I guess this is Edwin's way of telling us we won't be bothered until tomorrow."

Osiris folded himself into a sitting position next to Lane and took the lube from him. "I like that, but you don't have to feel like this means I expect anything from you."

Lane arched a brow. "You don't? Because I definitely expect you to fuck me eventually."

Osiris laughed. "I'd be happy to do that. I just meant that we don't have to do it tonight. I'm happy to wait."

Lane got to his knees and moved closer to Osiris. He took the lube back, but he didn't set it down. "What if I'm not?" he asked in a whisper.

Osiris was still smiling when Lane kissed him. There was no hesitation from either of them as they pressed together, and Lane liked that. He wanted things to be natural between them, and it felt that way.

He pushed Osiris back, and Osiris went without hesitation. It took some work, but eventually, Osiris was stretched out. Lane stayed back for a moment to admire the view. Osiris wore his usual flowy white pants, and they looked so damn good on him that Lane almost didn't want to take them off.

But he wanted to see Osiris's dick more than he wanted to stare at him dressed. He grinned as he hooked his fingers under the waistband and pulled. Osiris raised his hips to help, and Lane slid the pants down his legs. He wasn't surprised to see Osiris wasn't wearing anything under them, and he liked that. He liked having better access.

He dropped the pants to the side while Osiris took off his shirt. Lane was still dressed, but he'd started wearing the same things as everyone else in the palace, so getting rid of the comfortable light garments was easy. Then they were both naked, just the way Lane wanted them.

He leaned down and kissed Osiris's stomach. The head of Osiris's cock brushed against Lane's cheek, and he grinned at the wetness it left on his skin.

He was going to love this.

"I need to remember to thank Edwin tomorrow," Osiris said in a throaty voice.

Lane laughed and kissed Osiris's thigh. "I don't think he wants to know about our sex life."

"He knew what we'd be doing. He wouldn't have supplied the lube if he hadn't."

"Doesn't mean he wants details or to imagine us in this position." But maybe they could do something nice for him.

Tomorrow.

Lane opened his mouth and licked the length of Osiris's cock. Osiris grunted and reached for Lane's head but stopped before touching him. This was new for them, and they needed to find out what the other liked and wanted. When it came to hair-pulling during sex, Lane was all for it.

So he grabbed one of Osiris's hands and put it on his head. Osiris's fingers slipped into his hair, and Lane would have grinned if he hadn't been swallowing Osiris's cock down.

He tasted good—warm, slightly sweaty, but like home. Lane didn't understand how he could feel this way so soon after they met, but he didn't think it mattered.

He'd already known Osiris was it for him. No matter what happened with Apophis, he and Osiris would face it together.

Lane couldn't remember the last time he'd fully trusted

someone in this kind of situation, but he did trust Osiris. When Osiris tightened his hold on Lane's hair, Lane relaxed his mouth and throat and let him fuck his mouth. He wanted to feel owned and to know he was Osiris's. He wanted Osiris to brand him in whatever way possible.

Lane blindly searched for the lube. Osiris seemed to read his mind because he grinned and grabbed it, then pushed it into Lane's hand. Lane wrapped his fingers around it without pausing what he was doing with his mouth. He didn't know how long they had. Hopefully, it would be the entire night, but anything might happen to disturb them. The earthquakes were coming more often these days, and one of them might interrupt them.

He struggled with the bottle for a moment because it was still sealed, but it finally popped open. When it did, he slicked his fingers without looking down because he didn't want to waste even one second, then reached behind himself. Osiris made a strangled sound when he realized what Lane was doing, but he didn't try to stop him or intervene in any way. Out there, he was the one in control. He was the most powerful, the god everyone looked up to. Here, though? He was all Lane's.

Lane used every trick he remembered to push Osiris to the edge of pleasure, but he didn't let him come. That would only happen once he was inside Lane.

It would be the first time Lane had done this without protection. He knew Osiris would magic a condom out of thin air if he insisted, but they didn't need one. Gods weren't human. They didn't get ill, and they didn't have STDs. Not using a condom felt more intimate, but then, this was forever for Lane.

He kept his gaze up to be able to see how Osiris felt. For the first time, Osiris's cheeks were flushed, and Lane felt incredibly smug that it was because of him. Osiris wasn't looking Lane in the eyes. He was staring at Lane's ass, so he arched his back and raised it even more as he pushed his fingers inside himself to get ready for Osiris.

"You're so beautiful," Osiris murmured.

His voice held so many promises. Lane wanted him to keep every single one of them, and he wanted to make his own promises to Osiris. It didn't matter that they'd only met recently. Time didn't matter at all now that Lane was dead. He'd deliver on every promise he made, and he knew Osiris would do the same.

Osiris sat up, startling Lane, who let go of his cock. He stared at it for a moment. It was slick with his saliva, hard and flushed, and he wanted it inside.

Which seemed to be what Osiris wanted, too, because he grabbed Lane's arms and pulled him closer. Lane's fingers left his body as they rolled on the blankets. There wasn't much space on the balcony, but Osiris made it work. He was smiling when he finally got Lane on his back, and Lane could only smile back.

He wrapped his arms around Osiris's neck and opened his legs to welcome him. Osiris settled on top of him, fitting perfectly between Lane's legs. Lane hadn't expected anything different. From the first time he'd seen Osiris, he'd been drawn to him, almost like in those romance books his mother liked to read. Lane had stolen them often when he was a teenager, and he'd dreamed about being a vampire or a shifter's mate. He hadn't gotten that, and he'd stopped thinking about it when he'd grown up, but now he had something even better. He had a god, but more importantly, he had someone who wanted and loved him and would protect him.

It was so much better.

Osiris's cock bumped against Lane's, then slid under his balls, making him groan. He felt empty, and he needed Osiris to fill him up. He groaned, hoping Osiris would take the hint.

He had no problem being vocal about what he wanted, but he wasn't sure he could get a word out at the moment—or at least nothing that wasn't *yes* and *harder*.

"You're everything I could have dreamed of," Osiris whispered.

Lane pulled him closer. "Same. I didn't expect you when I died, but I think the best things in life are always unexpected." Although he hoped their lives would settle down eventually.

Osiris moved back and reached down to wrap his fingers around his cock. He aimed it at Lane's body, and Lane opened up, needing him inside. Lane had stretched himself as well and quickly as possible, but there was still a sting.

Good thing he enjoyed it.

Letting Osiris in was easy, especially when Osiris kissed Lane. Osiris sank into him completely, and Lane wrapped his legs around him, holding him in place and using his heels to press the two of them closer.

It wasn't perfect—there was something stuck under Lane's back that poked him every time Osiris thrust into him, and Lane's legs kept sliding off—but Lane wouldn't have wanted it any other way. It was real when everything else in his life still felt like a dream, and that was what he clung to as Osiris fucked him.

"This is real," he whispered. "You're real, and you're mine." That was almost impossible to believe.

"I've been yours since the day you came into my world."

Lane pressed his lips together. This wasn't the best moment to cry, not even from happiness. Instead, he pulled Osiris closer and kissed him with all he had and felt. He didn't think either of them was ready to say the three little words yet, but he knew how he felt.

As pleasure grew, Lane burrowed his face against Osiris's neck. He briefly wondered if maybe there was someone on their own balcony right now who could hear them, but he couldn't bring himself to care. The only thing that mattered was Osiris, the love between them that grew until they both came clutching the other as if they never wanted to let go. Lane knew he didn't and trusted that Osiris felt the same way.

Lane clung to Osiris as he finished shuddering through his orgasm. Osiris had to move eventually, and he slid out of Lane, leaving him feeling too empty. Osiris wasn't going anywhere, though. He grabbed one of the blankets and used its corner to clean Lane's stomach, then his ass, making Lane flush both with the pleasure of being taken care of and a hint of embarrassment.

When Lane first realized he'd died, he thought he'd lost everything, and he had. What he'd found was so precious that he couldn't find it in himself to regret what had happened. It didn't matter that the darkness was coming and that Apophis would no doubt try to destroy the world. The giant snake would have to deal with Lane if he thought for one second that he could take Osiris from him.

Chapter Ten

Osiris had many problems that needed a solution, and one of them was how to protect Lane better. He'd wanted Lane close and still did, but he wasn't blind. Every day, more demons came out, and more guards died. It had gotten to the point that Osiris would have to make a decision on whether or not he should seal off the palace. They could hide inside while the demons pounded on the doors, but it wouldn't last long.

He raked a hand through his hair and pulled on it. He needed to find a solution, but there wasn't anything he could do. Ra would have to be the one to defeat Apophis, with the help of as many gods as he could gather, and while Thoth was the god of magic and was still trying to find a way to fortify the darkness, so far, he was empty-handed.

Then, there was Osiris, who was supposed to protect the dead souls that still came in every day but couldn't even protect his guards. Soon, there wouldn't be enough of them to protect the palace, which would endanger everyone who lived there. Osiris had already asked as many souls as he could to leave, but there were still too many people around, including Lane and Barnaby.

He tapped his fingertips on his desk, knowing that Lane would probably hate him for doing this but feeling the need to do it anyway. He grabbed his phone and quickly dialed Ra's number, his heart racing at the thought that Ra might say no to his request.

Lane didn't want to move on, and he didn't want to go to

another underworld. His only request had been to stay with Osiris, but Osiris couldn't let him anymore. That meant finding him another place, possibly one where Osiris could reach him when they wanted to see each other.

The sky palace—as the boyfriend of one of the gods Osiris had become close to called it—was well protected. It would probably be the first place Apophis went once he was free, but Osiris doubted he'd be able to do much damage. After what had happened last time, the gods had made sure it would be a safe place for them to hide. That was probably why so many of them hadn't bothered to answer Ra's calls for help. They thought they'd be fine, and they probably would, but what about humanity? What about the many people who lived, loved, and died? They might not be Osiris's responsibility as long as they lived, but that didn't mean he didn't feel responsible for them.

"Osiris," Ra said when he answered. "Is everything all right?"

"I don't think anything is all right," Osiris said with a snort. "But Apophis is still where he should be. That's not why I called, at least not entirely. Can I talk to you for a moment, or am I disturbing you?"

"I'm listening."

Osiris sucked in a breath. "I need to find a safe place for Lane and his best friend. This palace isn't safe anymore, and while I know Lane will be angry at me for doing this behind his back, I couldn't live with myself if something were to happen to him or Barnaby."

"I'll admit I'm surprised you waited so long to ask. I thought you'd want to keep your human safe, but I didn't want to assume. Freddie told me to let the two of you talk things out, so I haven't asked."

"Freddie is a smart man. Unfortunately, there's nothing to talk about with Lane. He's already decided he wasn't going anywhere, and while I agreed, things are getting worse. I don't want him here when Apophis breaks out."

The silence was heavy. Osiris had just said what they both thought, and he took a moment to admit, at least to himself, that Apophis was coming back. It was just a matter of when.

"What do you want me to do?" Ra asked.

"Apophis will probably go straight to the sky palace when he breaks out, no doubt looking for you. It's still the best-protected place in the world, though, and I think Lane will be safe there."

"Why does everyone insist on calling it the sky palace?" Ra grumbled. "It's ridiculous."

His annoyed tone made Osiris smile, something he hadn't been doing enough of since this mess had started. Lane was the only thing that made him smile, but these days, even he wasn't enough.

"Lane has been calling it that, and I guess it's catching. It makes sense for the humans, though. They all live or lived in the human realm, and the palace where the gods live is something of a dream for them."

Ra sighed. "I'm aware. I can take Lane to the sky palace, but I won't force him into anything. You need to tell him and get his approval." He hesitated. "Maybe you could move, too."

Osiris took a moment to imagine what would happen if he did. Technically, nothing forbade him from visiting the sky palace or even moving back there. He was a god in the Egyptian pantheon and had as much right to do so as any other god, if not more. He might not be the most powerful god in the pantheon, but he was close.

But most of the gods had shunned him after he'd died and had become the god of the underworld, and that wasn't going to change anytime soon. There would be a scandal if he decided to move back, and he was tempted to say yes just because of that.

"My place is here," he told Ra. "I'm not abandoning my souls."

"I didn't think you would, but I still needed to ask. Have you managed to convince most of them to move on?"

"A few are resisting, but they're not the ones I'm worried about. People continue to die. I can't just accept all of them in the afterworld because I don't know if they deserve it, but having to check their hearts one by one is a lengthy process. It's one of the reasons I need to be here, but Lane doesn't have to be."

"Somehow, I doubt he'll see things that way." Ra sounded amused. "But if either of you changes their mind, there'll be a spot for you in the sky palace. And for your friend, of course. Just let me know after you've talked to Lane."

Osiris decided to do just that as soon as he and Ra had hung up. He left his office, ignoring Edwin's curious glance, and headed to the library. He knew that was where he'd find Lane, who'd been working with Barnaby to keep the gods helping with the demons fed and rested.

It had surprised Osiris, but he was proud of his human. Lane had decided to stay because he wanted to do his part, and he'd found something he could do.

But Osiris's place was here in the underworld, and while Lane's place was by his side, Osiris was unwilling to put him in danger. He couldn't force Lane to do anything, but that didn't mean he wasn't going to try to convince him. To him, Lane was the most important person in the world, and he'd burn everything down if it meant protecting him.

Lane knew he wouldn't like whatever Osiris had to say as soon as he saw Osiris's expression.

He and Barnaby had kept the library doors open, so Lane

had seen Osiris right away when he walked in. He'd been going over a list of supplies he and Barnaby needed to find, but he put it down and stared at his boyfriend from the chair he was sitting in. "What is it? Has something happened?" Surely, if Apophis had managed to escape, Lane would have felt it. He'd felt every earthquake, like everyone else in the underworld. When the darkness fell, it wouldn't be something they could ignore.

"I need to talk to you." Osiris looked over to Barnaby. "Both of you."

Yep. Lane wasn't going to like whatever was about to happen.

He and Barnaby exchanged a glance, and Lane settled back in his chair. Osiris didn't sit with them, instead opting to pace the length of the library. He seemed to need a moment to put his thoughts in order, which Lane was happy to give him. He'd give him so much more if he could, but unfortunately, he was only human.

Osiris eventually stopped in front of the table. "I called Ra. I asked him if moving both of you to the sky palace was possible. He agreed, so I need you to go pack your things."

Lane stared. There was no way Osiris had suggested what he'd just suggested, right? Because he and Lane had already talked about it, and Lane had made sure Osiris knew he wasn't going anywhere. This might not be his fight, but that didn't mean he wouldn't fight it. He couldn't do much, but he wasn't useless, and it was enough.

Or at least, it had been until now.

"Aren't you happy with the work we're doing?" he asked.

Osiris frowned as if he didn't understand. "Of course I am. You're taking care of us, and everyone is grateful for everything you do."

"Then why are you sending me away?"

"Because it's too dangerous to stay. I just had to tell the

wife of another guard that her husband had vanished forever. I don't want to lose you that way. I don't want to lose either of you."

Lane got to his feet. He didn't want to fight. He understood where Osiris was coming from, and if he was honest, he could admit that he'd do the same if their roles were reversed. He wanted to protect Osiris as much as Osiris wanted to protect him. He just didn't have the opportunity of sending Osiris far, far away.

"Isn't the sky palace the first place Apophis will go once he's free?" Barnaby asked. "I mean, Ra was the one who locked him up the first time around, right? Won't he want revenge?"

"I have no doubt that's where he'll go," Osiris confirmed. "But there's a reason most of the Egyptian gods live in the palace and hardly ever leave. After the first time Apophis rose to power, they knew they needed more protection. No matter how hard Apophis tries, he won't be able to destroy the sky palace. The gods who live there have made sure of that. He can rage in the human world for thousands of years without the gods having to worry about it."

Lane grimaced. "That's not a nice way to put it."

"That's because there's nothing nice about the situation. Apophis will want to throw the world into chaos, and the gods won't care enough to try to stop him. They'll watch him from their palace, knowing they're safe and that nothing will happen to them."

"And you want us to do the same?"

Osiris came to stand in front of Lane. "You'd never do that. I only want you to go to the sky palace because I need you to be safe. I have to know that Apophis won't be able to touch you."

"But he'll be able to touch you. He'll be able to hurt you, maybe even kill you." The thought was enough for Lane to feel breathless. "That's not something I can deal with. I'll only go to the sky palace if you come with me."

Osiris was already shaking his head. "I can't. I'm the god of the underworld, and my place is here. I'm needed to help the newly dead souls arriving every day, and if Apophis gets free, there will be even more of them. Someone must take care of them and ensure they get what they deserve in the afterlife."

"What do you think will happen if Apophis kills you?" Lane was sure Osiris had already thought about it, but they hadn't talked about it. "What will happen to the souls, then? Who will be there to watch their ceremony?"

Osiris rubbed his face. He looked tired, and since Lane slept next to him every night, he knew his boyfriend wasn't sleeping enough. He wished he could do something, but unfortunately, this was out of his reach.

He'd never expected to die, much less to end up dating a god. He'd certainly never expected to fall in love with a god.

But maybe that god needed to hear it.

"I realize you want me to leave because you're worried about me, and I understand it. *I* worry about *you*, though. I love you, which means I'll always worry about you, especially when I know you're in danger. I wish I could take you all the way to the sky palace and force you to stay there, but I can't do that, and you can't force me to go, either. You're afraid of losing me as much as I'm afraid of losing you. I won't give up on us and will be here to support you, whatever happens. I realize I'm not able to do much, but I'm doing everything I can. Even if the only thing I can do is be there for you at night when you come home distraught, that's what I want to do."

"I'm terrified of losing you," Osiris murmured.

Lane wanted to tell him everything would be okay, but he couldn't. He suspected it would be a lie, and he didn't want to lie to the man he loved. Instead, he pushed himself into

Osiris's arms, relieved when Osiris cinched his arms around him to hold him close. When he tilted his head up, Osiris kissed him, and Lane knew he'd surrendered.

Either they lived together, or they'd died together.

Lane still had hope that Thoth would find the right spell, or if Apophis got out, that Ra and the others would be able to stop him. He had once already, and now that he'd met Frey, he had an important reason to ensure that Apophis got what he deserved.

Someone cleared their throat, and Lane remembered that Barnaby had been with him in the library. He didn't push away from Osiris, but he put enough space between them that he could look at his friend.

Barnaby was biting his lower lip. He looked like he wasn't sure whether or not to say something, and Lane thought he knew what that something was.

"You should go," he said.

Barnaby frowned. "It's not that I want to leave you behind."

"You should be safe. I might not be in love with you, but you're my best friend, and I don't want anything to happen to you. You're not as stubborn as Osiris, so I was hoping you'd agree to go."

Barnaby's smile was tremulous. "I really want to see the sky palace. I know I said I was fine with dying and everything, but the past few weeks have shown me that there's more out there for me and that I deserve all of it."

"You do." Barnaby deserved everything he'd ever wanted.

A loud crack interrupted the conversation. Lane clutched Osiris's arms as the ground shook under them. The entire room was shaking, and several books dropped to the floor. Lane was getting used to the earthquakes, but he hated them. He hated what they meant and represented, and if he could, he'd walk straight into the darkness and tell Apophis to fucking stop it.

And then, he'd probably die. But, like Barnaby, Lane had realized that even though he was dead, there was still so much for him out there. He didn't want to miss even one of them.

He didn't want to miss one moment with Osiris.

Osiris could see Lane was freaking out, but there was nothing he could do for the man he loved. He was scared, too, even though he was a god. He could only imagine how much worse it was for Lane.

There was nothing either of them could do except wait for the end of the earthquake. Osiris tightened his hold on Lane, keeping him close as he leaned against the table. Their entire world was shaking, and for a moment, Osiris wondered if something was about to break. The first thing that came to mind was the palace, but there was also the darkness to consider. Between the demons poking at it any chance they got, Apophis's ally doing his best to get Apophis out, and the many earthquakes, it wouldn't be a surprise to find out the darkness had finally fallen.

The earthquake felt like it lasted forever, even though it couldn't have been more than a few seconds. When it ended, Osiris stayed where he was for a moment, breathing in Lane's scent and waiting to see what would happen next. This time, there were no servants running in the hallways. Everyone knew what the earthquakes were and that nothing could be done about them. Osiris would already have done it if there was.

"Looks like it's over," Barnaby eventually said.

He sounded scared, but Osiris would have been surprised if he hadn't been. Everyone ought to be scared at the thought of Apophis breaking out of the darkness.

Osiris took a step back from Lane but kept his hands on Lane's shoulders. Lane's eyes were wide, but he was clearly trying not to appear scared. Osiris wanted to reassure him, but he needed to check in with Edwin. He'd be the first to know if something had happened outside or inside of the palace, and Osiris had to be the second so they could solve whatever problems this last earthquake had created.

"Are the two of you okay?" he asked.

Lane nodded. "I'm fine."

"I'm fine, too, but if your offer still stands, I think I'm going to go pack my stuff," Barnaby said. He shuddered and wrapped his arms around himself. "No offense, but I don't want to spend one more second here."

"Go pack," Osiris told him. He understood how Barnaby felt, and if he had the opportunity, he would have packed and left, too. "Come to me as soon as you're done, and I'll call Ra."

Barnaby nodded and rushed out. Osiris watched him for a moment, wishing that both he and Lane could follow him. But his place was here, and clearly, Lane thought that his place was next to him.

That didn't mean Osiris wasn't terrified for Lane. He wanted him to be close, and he was relieved Lane had decided not to leave, but at the same time, he was worried. It would be too easy for Apophis to hurt Lane, and that wasn't something Osiris could live with.

But he was going to have to accept it. There was no changing Lane's mind, just like there was no changing their situation. Ra was talking to every god he could find, both from their pantheon and outside of it, gathering an army. Thoth was still working on his books, researching every spell he could find to try to find one that would seal the darkness.

And Osiris was here, unable to protect his people. Unable to protect Lane.

But if Apophis ever tried touching Lane, Osiris would be

there, standing between them, even if it meant final death for him.

CHAPTER ELEVEN

"I have it!"

The voice made Osiris jump. He turned to glare at Thoth only for his brain to understand what Thoth had said. "You have what?" Osiris asked, afraid to be wrong.

Thoth was holding a piece of paper that he slammed onto Osiris's desk. "A spell to strengthen the darkness."

Osiris got to his feet. "When can you do it? What do you need?"

"I already gathered everything. We can go out right now." Thoth hesitated. "But it's only a patch. It won't hold Apophis inside indefinitely. It also won't defeat him."

Osiris had barely expected Thoth to find this spell, let alone a spell to defeat Apophis. It would have been great, but they needed to make do with what they had, and this was better than nothing.

Much better.

"It's fine. If you can do this spell now, we should head out. I'll let Edwin know what's going on so he can contact the others."

"I can't promise it'll work. I'm pretty sure it was used to fix patches in the darkness when it was first created, but the language is archaic, and even though I did my best to translate it, it might not be precise enough to help as much as we need it to."

Osiris grabbed Thoth's shoulder and squeezed. "This is better than we could have expected. At this point, anything will help. Thank you for doing this."

"My life is at risk, too, if Apophis comes out. This is entirely selfish."

But Osiris didn't think it was. Thoth loved books and his studies, so he would have done this even if he hadn't been involved because of his thirst for knowledge, but he also didn't want anything to happen to the people he loved. Osiris didn't know if he was one of those people, but they were family and worked well together. He'd do whatever he could to save Thoth, and he suspected the same went for Thoth.

"Ready?" he asked.

Thoth nodded. "The sooner we do this, the better. I'm just praying it's not too late."

Osiris hadn't wanted to say it out loud, but neither of them could deny it was a possibility.

But they needed time, and if this spell gave it to them, it would be worth it. Even if it was only one day, maybe two, it would be one or two days more they'd have to get ready to face Apophis.

They left the office. Edwin was at his desk, and Osiris stopped to tell him to contact Ra. Edwin's eyes were wide as he nodded, and Osiris could see the hope in them. Like everyone else, Edwin needed this to go well. He still refused to leave the palace, although Osiris wasn't done trying to convince him. He'd already lost too many people. He wasn't going to lose anyone else, especially not Edwin—or Lane.

Osiris hadn't noticed that Thoth was carrying a bag on his shoulder. It probably contained what he needed to do the spell, and while Osiris was tempted to ask, he wasn't sure he'd understand. He wasn't studious like Thoth. He also didn't care what was in the bag as long as it worked.

They left the palace behind. They didn't take any guards, because Osiris was unwilling to put anyone else in danger. The guards were already doing too much, and he didn't want to lose any more of them. He realized he would when

Apophis broke out of the darkness, but for now, he'd keep them safe the best he could. That meant keeping them in the palace and away from the darkness, even though several of them had offered to come with Osiris and Thoth when they'd walked by.

They were silent as they walked. Osiris visited the darkness daily, keeping an eye on it and ensuring it was still in one piece. He didn't have the same kind of magic Thoth had, though, so he didn't fully know how bad it had gotten. As they reached the edge of the darkness, one glance at Thoth's expression was enough for him to understand.

Thoth stopped at the edge and raised a hand to touch the darkness. He shivered, a grimace appearing on his face. "I can feel it," he murmured.

"And I don't think it's pleasant from your expression."

"It's not. It feels thick and oily, almost as if it's the consistency that keeps Apophis in." Thoth licked his lips. "It's so much weaker than it should be. I don't know how much good the spell will do, to be honest."

"Even if it only buys us one more day, it'll be enough," Osiris promised.

Thoth didn't look convinced, but he put down his bag and started taking out things. Osiris wanted to watch, but instead, he gazed around, ensuring they were alone. He wouldn't be surprised if demons tried to stop them. If they did, he'd be ready for them.

Everything was quiet until Thoth started the spell. When he did, the air prickled Osiris's skin. He could *feel* the magic, and he wasn't the only one. As Thoth started chanting, his hands raised toward the darkness, Osiris heard a grunt. He turned to face a demon, extracting his sword as he moved.

He kept the demon as far away from Thoth as possible so it wouldn't bother him, but it became more difficult when the number of demons rose. Then it became even worse because a god appeared in the demons' midst.

Osiris didn't recognize him, but he didn't have to in order to know who he was. He'd heard all about Maahes, including how Ra had cut off his hand the last time they'd faced each other, so he wasn't surprised to see the other god only had one hand, but in the one he still had, he carried a sword.

That wasn't the worrying part, though. No, the worrying part was the dozens of demons standing behind him.

Osiris glanced at Thoth, who was too busy to have noticed what was happening. He hoped that after getting Edwin's message, Ra would come. Maybe he would, but it would be too late. These demons wanted Thoth away from the darkness, and considering how many were there, they'd eventually succeed.

But Osiris wouldn't let them pass without a fight. He raised his sword and faced Maahes, ready to kick his ass.

Even if it was the last thing he did.

Maahes screamed and threw himself at Osiris. The demons behind him moved at the same time, and while Osiris did his best, he was only one god. Eventually, the demons reached Thoth. One of them jumped onto Thoth's back, and the chanting stopped. Thoth made a strangled sound. Osiris rushed to his side, pulling the demon off his back, but it was too late.

Thoth's eyes were wide as he stared at Osiris, blood pouring from his throat. The demon had raked its claws along Thoth's skin, probably to ensure Thoth couldn't continue chanting. Thoth wouldn't die from it, but he'd need time to heal, and they didn't have that time.

Osiris cut down the demon who'd hurt Thoth. Thoth slumped onto the ground, both of his hands clutching his throat. A piercing pain hit Osiris in the shoulder, and he looked down to see that a sword had cut through him. This wasn't a lethal wound, either, but it hurt like a bitch.

He swung his sword as he turned. Maahes grinned, clearly

happy about the outcome of his incursion. Unfortunately, he was probably right to be. There were too many demons for Osiris and Thoth to push back, and with the wound in Thoth's throat, he couldn't continue the spell.

There was only one thing Osiris could do. He turned to face Maahes with his sword held high. At the same time, he stepped toward Thoth, who was struggling to get to his feet. He was pushing through the pain, which was what Osiris needed him to do.

As soon as Osiris was next to Thoth, he grabbed him, and with one last glance at Maahes, he got them out of there.

Lane screeched when two people suddenly appeared in front of him in the middle of the library. One of the figures slumped to the floor, and Lane's brain had trouble making sense of what he was seeing. Logically, he knew that the liquid pouring down Thoth's throat was blood, but he didn't understand.

Why was Thoth wounded? Was he dying? A human would have died from that kind of wound, but Thoth wasn't human.

Then there was Osiris. He was bleeding, too, dark red staining his white shirt. He didn't seem to care because he was already bending over Thoth to get him to his feet again.

"What happened?" Lane asked, rushing around the table where he'd be sitting to reach the two.

"Thoth found a spell," Osiris explained. He hauled Thoth into his arms.

Lane sucked in a breath. "To strengthen the darkness? Is that what the two of you were doing?"

He followed Osiris into the hallway. Osiris knew where he was going, and Lane wanted answers. He didn't want to push, considering Thoth's state, but he needed to know.

"It was only supposed to be a patch, but he didn't have the time to finish it. We were attacked."

"You should have waited for us," a voice boomed at the end of the hallway.

Osiris glared and continued carrying Thoth. "I thought you'd be here faster," he told Ra.

Neither of them hesitated. Ra had been coming toward them, but now that he was with them, he fell into step with Osiris. Lane trailed behind them, not knowing what to do. He had so many questions, but he wasn't sure he should ask them. Besides, he suspected Osiris was about to tell them everything, anyway.

"I told my assistant to let you know what was happening," Osiris said.

Lane stared at the floor. They were leaving a trail of blood, and he swallowed thickly, not wanting to think about what it might mean. Thoth was a god. They were immortal, or at least, they were supposed to be. Lane knew the stories about some of them dying, but usually, it was a god who'd done the killing, not a demon. Thoth had to be all right, even though it didn't look like it.

"I got his message and came as soon as I could, but I was talking to someone." Ra leaned closer to Thoth. "Will he be all right?"

"I don't know. I hope he'll heal fast, because the demons are out there, probably pounding the darkness down as we're talking. They weren't alone this time."

Ra sighed. "Maahes."

"Unless there's another one-handed god running around trying to free Apophis, yes. He was there."

They finally reached a set of doors. Ra hurried to open them, and Osiris walked inside. For a moment, Lane wondered if Osiris would take Thoth to a healer, but he wasn't surprised to see they were in what had to be Thoth's rooms. Instead of going toward the bed like Lane would have expected, Osiris moved deeper into the suite. When Lane followed, he realized it was because he wanted to put Thoth into the bathtub.

Well, it was more like a pool, but at least like this, there wouldn't be blood everywhere. Although it was already too late for that considering the trail they'd left in the hallways.

Osiris dug into his pants and took out his phone. He winced, which reminded Lane that he was wounded, too. He'd hoped it was Thoth's blood, but now that he was closer, his stomach churned at the sight of a raw wound under the white shirt Osiris was still wearing.

"Get the healer to Thoth's rooms now," Osiris ordered before hanging up the phone.

He'd probably called Edwin, who wouldn't mind the tone Osiris had used as soon as he found out what had happened. Usually, he was easy to snap when Osiris treated him like a servant, but Thoth might be dying.

Lane wasn't a hundred percent sure of that, but it certainly looked like that was what was happening. He didn't know Thoth well, mostly because the god kept to himself and focused on his books and research, but he'd spent some time with him and liked him. It didn't matter that he did, though. Thoth didn't deserve any of this. *None* of them deserved any of this. It was all Apophis's fault, and Lane had the sudden and stupid urge to march to the darkness and yell at the asshole snake.

But instead, as soon as Osiris hung up, Lane was on him. He was afraid to hurt him more than he already was, but he pulled away the shirt from the wound, trying to get a better look.

Osiris hissed and caught Lane's wrist. Lane froze, but thankfully, Osiris didn't push him away.

Instead, his shoulders slumped. "I'm fine," he promised.

"That wound doesn't look fine." It was still bleeding, and from what Lane could see of it, it had been made by a massive blade.

"Maahes stabbed me with his sword," Osiris explained.

Lane swallowed. "He stabbed you with a sword."

"I was distracted because Thoth had been hurt. I had my back to Maahes, and he took advantage."

Lane didn't want any details. He just needed Osiris to be all right, and right now, that wasn't the case.

"We need to head out," Ra declared.

Lane almost told him to fuck off since it was obvious Osiris wasn't going anywhere. His jaw dropped when instead of telling him just that, Osiris nodded.

"We can go now. Edwin knows what's happening, and I'm sure that once Thoth is awake, he'll give him more details. I left too many demons out there."

"I've already contacted the others, and they're coming," Ra informed them.

Lane felt like he was going nuts. "You can't go out there," he snapped. "You're wounded."

Osiris's expression was gentle when he turned to Lane but also steely, and Lane knew he wouldn't win this fight.

"I'll be fine," Osiris promised. "I'm a god. Besides, I'm already dead. That makes me doubly immortal."

Lane knew nothing he could do or say would stop Osiris. His boyfriend was stubborn, and in this case, he probably was right to be. Considering what had just happened, someone needed to keep an eye on the demons, and Osiris was the best person to do so. "I don't think it works that way," Lane grumbled.

"I don't know, but I have to do this. Will you stay with Thoth?"

"You don't even have to ask. Go, and come back in one piece."

Osiris nodded. "I'll do my best."

Lane only realized what he'd said after Osiris had left.

He'd told him to come back in one piece when he'd known that when Osiris's brother had killed him, he'd cut him up in several pieces and had hidden them around. He was a massive idiot. But he was also a panicky idiot, so hopefully, Osiris would forgive him.

Lane had no idea what to do, so he sat on the bench by the wall once the healer arrived. The healer had several assistants with him, and Edwin was there, too, hovering close by. Lane knew he wanted an explanation, but Lane didn't have the strength. His entire focus was on Osiris and what might be happening to him right now, and he felt as if he tried talking, he'd break down, which was the last thing he needed.

"We'll be all right," Edwin whispered.

He was staring at Thoth, but Lane heard the words anyway. "I hope so," he whispered back. He didn't know what he'd do if something were to happen to Osiris. Lane wasn't ready to face Apophis yet. He didn't think he'd *ever* be ready to face Apophis, but it looked like he wouldn't have a choice. When it happened, though, he wanted to be with Osiris. He trusted Ra to keep Osiris safe, but that didn't mean he wasn't terrified.

Unfortunately for him, he didn't have a choice in any of this. Osiris was the god of the underworld, and he was ready to defend his people and his realm to his last breath.

And it might just come to that.

EPILOGUE

Lane stared at the figure in the bed. He wished he could do more for Thoth, who'd been unconscious for days. The healer had tried reassuring Lane and told him it was entirely normal. Even though Thoth was a god, his body had gone through a shocking experience, and he'd lost a massive amount of blood. It would take him some time to regenerate, but once he did, he'd be as good as new.

Or at least, that was what the healer insisted would happen.

Lane wanted to believe him, but Thoth still in his bed and so pale that every time Lane visited, he freaked out a little more. He just wanted Thoth to open his eyes, dammit. He didn't even care about Apophis and the spell, though he should. Ra and Osiris had gotten rid of most of the demons that had been hanging around the darkness that day, but Maahes, the man helping Apophis, had fled. Lane wanted to hunt him down himself, but considering he was human while Maahes was a god, he'd probably get killed.

Once again, he was powerless. There was nothing he could do to help, no matter how much time he spent standing by Thoth's bed. He wished Barnaby were here to distract him, but his friend had left after the earthquake, and Lane wasn't about to call him to whine about needing a distraction. Barnaby was in the sky palace, safe and sound, and Lane wanted things to stay that way.

A strong arm wrapped around Lane's shoulders. Lane leaned against Osiris, needing his strength.

"He'll be all right," Osiris promised.

"Both you and the healer have been saying that for days now."

"We know what we're talking about. It's not the first time I've seen a god hurt the way Thoth was. He'll be fine eventually."

Lane sighed. This was one more thing in which he needed to trust Osiris, and he did. He just didn't like the waiting pattern they were in.

When Ra and Osiris had reached the darkness that day, they'd been relieved to see it was still intact. It was weaker than ever, but with Thoth unconscious, there was nothing anyone could do. Even having the spell Thoth had found, he was the only one who knew enough about magic to do something with it. They were waiting for him to wake up so he could go out there and do the spell, but Lane was starting to lose hope. He wanted Thoth to wake up, but he doubted it would happen in time.

He would never be lucky that way.

Back when he'd been alive, he'd always thought that in the case of a zombie apocalypse, he'd be one of the first to die. He didn't have it in him to survive that kind of situation, and honestly, he wasn't sure he'd *want* to survive it. This situation wasn't anywhere close to a zombie apocalypse, but it had the same urgency and fear, and it was hard to deal with it. Sometimes, Lane wanted to scream. Most of the time, he wanted to hide away in his room and never come out. Maybe if he ignored Apophis, the giant snake would never come out of the darkness.

Lane almost snorted at his thoughts. Of course Apophis would come out.

Lane's phone vibrated. He stepped away from Thoth's bed, smiling when he saw Barnaby's face on the screen. He'd taken the picture right after he and Barnaby had moved closer to

Osiris's suite. Barnaby had been beaming, and Lane cherished this picture.

"How did you know I needed to talk to you?" he asked as he answered.

"Best friend radar. What's going on?" Barnaby asked.

Lane sighed. He was in the hallway now, but Osiris was still inside, so Lane leaned against the wall to wait for him. "It's a mess. Thoth is still unconscious, and there's no one else who can help with the spell. We were so close, and now, we're further than ever from a solution."

Barnaby hummed. "But you said that even if Thoth had managed to do the spell, it wouldn't have worked forever."

"It wouldn't have, but we'd have been able to keep Apophis where he was for a while longer, hopefully long enough to find a way out of this."

"Honestly, I don't think there's a way out of this. We all want to believe there is, but at this point, the only outcome is a fight."

That was what Lane had been thinking, but he'd refused to admit it so far. He couldn't do that anymore. He had to accept what was in front of him, make his peace with it, and try to find a solution so that both he and Osiris, along with everyone they cared about, made it out alive.

"I don't know what to do," he confessed.

Barnaby sighed. "We both know there's not a lot you *can* do, and that's okay. It's not your job to solve this problem."

"It might not be, but I live here. If I want to survive, I might need to get my hands dirty."

"Or you might need to come to the sky palace. I know you don't want to leave Osiris behind, but maybe he could come with you. It's clear that Apophis is coming out whether we want it or not. The two of you will be safer here."

"He says no every time I mention it, although he offered to move me there."

Barnaby snorted. "Did he really think you'd say yes?"

"Possibly." Just like Lane was still hoping Osiris would say yes to moving there with him. But both of them were stubborn, and they both had their reason to say no.

Osiris wouldn't leave the underworld because his place was here. He wanted to protect his people, which was entirely understandable, even though Lane wasn't sure there was a way to protect anyone from Apophis and his demons. As for Lane, he wasn't leaving Osiris behind. He didn't care what happened to him as long as Osiris was all right. He'd defend the god he loved with his bare hands if he had to. He was pretty sure that only using his hands would barely tickle a demon, but he was ready to try anyway.

A loud crack made him jump. He looked around frantically, already knowing what was happening. He pressed harder against the wall as the earth started shaking under him.

"Lane?" Barnaby asked, but his voice sounded distant. Lane was still clutching the phone with his hand, but he'd lowered it and was pressing as much of his body as possible against the wall to stay on his feet, including the back of the hand holding the phone.

A crash inside the room made him jump. Osiris appeared at the open door, frantic until his gaze stopped on Lane. Then, he moved toward Lane, but the shaking made his legs unsteady. He had to hold himself up against the wall like Lane was.

Lane was pretty sure this was the strongest earthquake yet, and a sensation of doom filled him. There was no way Apophis wouldn't escape after this. Hell, the earth was still shaking, and the sound of things falling and breaking filled Lane's years.

Then Osiris was there, wrapping his arms around Lane and pulling him close. He pressed his body against Lane's and locked him against the wall, and Lane hugged him, keeping the two of them together. Osiris was protecting him, and while there wasn't much he could do, Lane was doing his best not to panic.

He wasn't sure he was doing a good job. Even being here at the palace, he knew what was happening, and Osiris's dire expression told Lane he wasn't the only one.

"Lane!" Barnaby's tiny voice came from the phone.

Lane raised it to his ear, afraid Barnaby would do something stupid like coming down if he didn't answer. "I'm here."

"What the fuck is happening?"

The ground finally slowed down, then stopped moving. It felt like it was still shaking, and Lane realized that it was his legs. "Another earthquake," he explained.

"That can't be good."

Lane doubted it had been.

As soon as the floor stopped moving, Osiris pushed away from Lane. He wanted nothing more than to stay with Lane, but a sinking feeling at the center of his stomach told him he needed to check on the darkness. This had been the strongest earthquake he'd ever felt, and with the darkness so weak, he wouldn't be surprised to find out it had broken.

He didn't have to go far to get confirmation. The sound of someone running toward them made him tense, and he placed himself between Lane in the direction from which the footsteps were coming. A guard appeared at the end of the hallway, and before Osiris could ask him if something had happened, he already had an answer. The guard's expression was enough for him to know.

Still, against all odds, Osiris hoped that something had broken in the palace. If it was something they could fix, he wouldn't have to worry about Apophis just yet.

"What?" he asked.

"It's the darkness," the guard said as he panted. "It has fallen. The guards in that area are gone, and the demons are coming."

"Apophis?"

The guard stared at Osiris with wide eyes. "The serpent is free."

Osiris was frozen for a moment. He'd known this would happen, but knowing it and having it happen was different. Was the serpent coming for the palace? "The demons are coming?"

"From what we could find out before the guards vanished, another crack opened at the foot of the darkness. It's what took it down, and demons are pouring through it. They're coming toward the palace, but we can't see them yet."

"Pull back everyone in the area. We need to barricade the palace. Evacuate everyone who isn't here to fight."

The guard nodded and ran away, and Osiris turned to Lane.

Apparently, he was predictable because Lane glared at him, his arms crossed over his chest. He had his stubborn expression on, which told Osiris that his suggestion wouldn't be welcome.

"You need to go to the sky palace," he still tried.

"As long as you're coming with me."

"I can't. Apophis is free, and demons are about to attack the palace. My people need me."

"And *you* need *me*. I'm not going anywhere without you, Osiris. If you die, I die."

"While the two of you are being dramatic, I went to find Ra," Barnaby's voice came from the phone Lane was still holding.

Osiris was grateful. He'd made a list of things to do if

Apophis ever broke out of the darkness, but he was utterly lost.

"We're coming up," he told Barnaby.

Lane's expression turned mulish. "You're not dumping me in the sky palace before coming back down here," he said.

"I don't know what will happen, but we need to talk to the others."

"What about Thoth?"

"We're taking him with us. We'll leave him there." Osiris hoped he'd be able to convince Lane to stay, too, but something told him he wouldn't. Thinking of the man he loved being attacked by demons was enough to send him into a fit of panic, but it was something he'd have to deal with. He wouldn't force Lane to do anything. They were in this together, no matter how terrifying it was.

Osiris held out his hand, and Lane stared at it for a moment. He took it, though, and Osiris breathed easier.

Together, they went back inside Thoth's room. His condition hadn't changed, but Osiris let go of Lane's hand to pick him up. Once Lane was touching his arm, he quickly took the three of them to the sky palace.

This time, no one complained about his presence. He wasn't even sure they noticed. He'd appeared in front of Nu's suite, and there were people running around, almost as if they knew what had happened. Osiris didn't know much about what Apophis was doing right now, which was one reason he needed to return as soon as possible. First, though, he had to make sure Thoth was safe.

The doors to Nu's suite were open, and Osiris quickly walked through. He wasn't surprised to see that most of the group had gathered there. Ra looked regal in his traditional armor, holding his sword. Freddie was next to him, his expression grim.

"Put him on the couch," Nu ordered, gesturing at Osiris.

Osiris obeyed. There was a sense of urgency with every movement he made, as if he was wasting time.

Once he was sure Thoth was as comfortable as possible, he turned to face the others. He recognized most of the faces and was glad to see Ra had managed to gather more gods than they'd expected. It wasn't all of them by any means, and many of the most powerful ones were missing, but it was a start.

He cleared his throat. "The darkness has fallen. Apophis is free."

And every single one of them would have to fight. There was no way to know how it would end or who would win, but no one here would ever stop trying. They were the last bastion the world had, and they couldn't fail.

Apophis was free, but if Osiris had anything to say about it, it wouldn't be for long.

And this time, he wouldn't give Apophis the opportunity to come back.

About the Author

Catherine is the creator of several series, most of them paranormal, including the Whitedell Pride Series and the Gillham Pack Series. While she graduated in translation, she decided to go the writer's way because it was more fun to create her own stories and characters.

She's been living in Italy for more than twenty years, but she's a daughter of the North—Belgium to be precise—and she misses it so much that she's already planning to move back.

She loves pizza—probably too much—her son, her pets, and of course, books. She sneaks some reading time into her schedule every time she has five minutes free from writing, demands from her various pets and son, and lastly, house work.

Connect with her:

lievens.catherine@gmail.com
BookBub: https://www.bookbub.com/authors/catherine-lievens
Website: https://authorcatherinelievens.com/
Facebook: https://www.facebook.com/catherine.lievens.9
Facebook Group: https://www.facebook.com/groups/411788002341528/
Twitter: https://twitter.com/authorCLievens
Newsletter: http://eepurl.com/c-uvKn